MISCHIEF, DEA
THE IDYLLIC W
BERMUDIAN BO

Fried White Grunts follows the fascinating adventures and misadventures of a young boy and his Hill Gang, a little group of kids who live on one of the highest hills on the island paradise of Bermuda. But all is not idyllic in their childhood world as death, mischief and the innocence of youth intertwine, thrusting them into the reality of loss and the promise of hope.

I was six years old when we hanged David Robinson.
If it hadn't been for the Durango Kid we probably never would have done it. As it was, it wasn't much fun anyway because he just went right along with it, and you have to admit that a hanging probably isn't as interesting if the person you're hanging just goes along with it. But David was like that — easy going and compliant, ready to oblige all the time, just wanting to be one of the gang.
Which is why he died.

"...This lively book gives you insight into the time, the place, and the curious way that boys' minds work. It is filled with telling details and crisp dialogue that will keep you reading."—***Elaine McCluskey, award-winning author of 'Hello Sweetheart' and 'Valerie the Great.'***

"...There's sweetness in this book, and stories of kindness ... lots of laughs and there's tragedy too — one awful event no one will ever forget. Colin Duerden writes deftly, and either he has an astonishing memory, or he's just really creative, or both ... beautifully written, and I wanted it to go on and on. But ... it ends and you'll be indignantly saying 'yes, yes but THEN what happened?' "—*Dr. Nancy White, Singer, Songwriter, Co-author of the hit musical 'Anne and Gilbert.'*

"...stories of the Hill Gang capture adventure and boyish bravado and at the same time, touch our souls with their innocence in the face of loss. A very enjoyable read- both heartfelt and humorous."—*Diana Whalen, Former Deputy Premier and Minister of Justice, Nova Scotia, Canada.*

"Welcome to a hill in the Bermuda of yesteryear and to heart-warming stories of the children whose home it was. By turns both funny and achingly poignant, we follow this endearing little band of characters as they learn all about life and perhaps also a little about death."—*Martin Buckley - Manager, The Bookmart at Brown & Co., Hamilton, Bermuda.*

"...moving tale of mostly pre-teen boys ... no more about such boys than are Twain's Huck and Tom books.
In every way that matters, Fried White Grunts is a grown up book by a grown up man."—*Terry Todd, Professor, University of Texas at Austin, Texas.*

FRIED WHITE GRUNTS
F. Colin Duerden

Moonshine Cove Publishing, LLC
Abbeville, South Carolina U.S.A.

This book is a work of fiction. Names, characters, places and incidents are products of the author's imagination or are used fictitiously. Any resemblance to actual events, locales or persons, living or dead, is entirely coincidental.

ISBN: 978-1-945181-207
Library of Congress PCN: 2017912930
Copyright 2017 by F. Colin Duerden

Front cover design by Carol MacNutt; cover and interior design by Moonshine Cove staff.

ABOUT THE AUTHOR

Colin was born and raised in Bermuda, and left there after graduating from high school to attend Dalhousie  University in Canada, where he obtained a Bachelor of Science degree and a Ph.D in Oceanography. He is the author of the award-winning international thriller *Bloodwater*, and his short story "Blame it on the Durango Kid" was an award winner in Atlantic Canada's Annual Writing Competition. This short story was subsequently published by Bookstogonow of Seattle, Washington, and has been incorporated as a chapter in *Fried White Grunts*. He is a Principal in an environmental management consulting firm, and spends far too little time sailing and writing, his two favorite passions. The author's website is:

Colinduerden.weebly.com

For Ryan, Josephine and Seth

Acknowledgment

I owe a big thank you to Rebecca Gillis and Jonny Chubbs, two of my favorite critics, for their valued input and enthusiastic support; to Nelson and Mary Ferguson, who've been 'grappled' for decades, and to the always available staff at Moonshine Cove for their expert advice and assistance.

"Those friends thou hast and their adoption tried, grapple them unto thy soul with hoops of steel."

—William Shakespeare, *Hamlet*

FRIED WHITE GRUNTS

Chapter 1
Blame it on the Durango Kid

I was six years old when we hanged David Robinson.

If it hadn't been for the *Durango Kid* we probably never would have done it. As it was, it wasn't much fun anyway because he just went right along with it, and you have to admit that a hanging probably isn't as interesting if the person you're hanging just goes along with it. But David was like that — easy going and compliant, ready to oblige all the time, just wanting to be one of the gang. Which is why he died.

David was really a boring victim when you get right down to it. I guess it has something to do with the fact that when you're six years old you haven't really gotten a good appreciation of the concept of death and all the implications that go along with it.

There were four of us — my cousin Stan, who was nine and big, about the size of a full grown adult, or so it seemed to us; Jackie, who was ten and pretty much of a midget even then, being only about as tall as David and me but very stocky and kind of bright, as a lot of small people seem to be. Jimmy was Jackie's brother. We called him Jay Jay and he was small and skinny and if we didn't have David we might have considered hanging him, except for his comic book collection.

Jay Jay had the biggest collection of comic books in the neighbourhood and he kept them in a big trunk in his bedroom and treated them like they were money. They were hard to get hold of and if he was mad at you then you'd never get near his room, much less his comic books. And how long could a normal kid go without an *Archie, Superman* or *Wonder Woman* fix*?* For sure we weren't going to jeopardize our entertainment future just to hang Jay Jay.

You have to remember that this was Bermuda before television, and the radio had programs like *Second Spring* and *Housewives Choice*. So you can understand the politics of the situation. Besides, we let Jay Jay bribe us with the loan of ten comic books of our choice if he could take part in the hanging.

The reason we were hanging David was because he was a Cowboy and we were Indians. We captured him because he was the smallest and the slowest in his posse of four Cowboys. The reason the other Cowboys didn't stay around to try and rescue him was because they all went home to lunch, which was a higher priority than saving David.

I was glad we'd decided that David should be a Cowboy the day we hanged him because otherwise it might have been me, given I was as small as Jay Jay and he had a bye because of the comic books.

But this time David's mother allowed him to play with us again, which was a very big thing for her because it meant that maybe she'd put the kite incident behind her. For the longest while she wouldn't let him near us, not since we tied him to the string of Stan's big kite on a windy day to see if he'd get pulled any distance.

David, as I said, was really quite small and the kite was really quite big and the wind was really quite gusty, as it can get on a small island like Bermuda. Especially if you're up on one of the highest hills. One of those gusts came along just after we'd attached David to the string and for a while he was airborne.

David's mother happened to be looking out of her kitchen window when he passed by and she got very upset. But by the time she got to him the wind had died down and he was only being dragged along a little bit. Anyway, for the longest time he wasn't allowed to be with us because, as she explained to us that day with her face all red and her eyes all angry-looking and her voice barely above a whisper, she didn't trust us to play safely and keep him out of harm's way.

But she either relented or forgot and here was David now, happy to be with us, happy to be the center of attention, and happy to offer his life as a sacrifice to us Indians. We usually tied our captives up for an hour or two and then set them free after they swore an oath of loyalty to the Indian chief. Stan was the Indian chief because he was the biggest and the oldest and the bravest.

I think it was Jackie who suggested the hanging. He'd seen one in a *Durango Kid* serial on Saturday at the Opera House matinee and it was still fresh in his mind. Not that anyone ever died in those serials but there was enough there to plant the seed. We talked about Jackie's suggestion for a few minutes, reached unanimous agreement in short order and David went willingly to the gallows, in this case the grey remains of a stunted and dead cedar tree.

We had an old piece of hemp rope that was once used to tie up our pet nanny goat. The nanny goat got loose from the rope for about the sixth time, but this last time she ate everything she could find in my auntie's garden. She was so upset because she used to spend a lot of time and water on her garden and in Bermuda during the growing season water can sometimes be a rare commodity. Anyway, she made my uncle promise to do something to make sure it never happened again. Never again!

My uncle asked our next door neighbour Mr. Hunt to do something about the goat so that what it did 'never happened again'. So Mr. Hunt got drunk on Gosling's Black Seal Rum and ginger beer and went about the job of solving the problem.

We were forbidden to watch what Mr. Hunt was going to do with respect to the problem. We were told to go in the house and stay there. But we knew just by the tone of the voices and the looks passing around that the nanny goat was in serious trouble, and we wanted to see what was going to be done with her.

We thought the punishment would be a beating on the bum with an oleander branch and then a muzzle or something that she'd have to wear to stop her from eating gardens. So we sneaked out of the house and hunkered down in the bushes in the backyard and watched Mr. Hunt beat our nanny goat to death with a ball peen hammer and a pickaxe.

We watched it all because we couldn't not watch, and it was a long time before I could sleep through the night without hearing the awful bleating as she was hit. What was even worse was the dull thud of the hammer as it slammed down on her head. I heard it over and over and I saw the blood pouring from her nose and mouth. But the most frightening thing, worse than the sound of the blows or the sight of the blood, was her eyes. Huge, sad eyes, eyes that looked into my eyes and I thought they held a plea, until another blow of the hammer or the axe, I can't remember which, and her eyes closed and never opened again. But at night when she came into my dreams her eyes never closed. I saw them then. Sometimes I see them now.

So that's why we had the rope we used to hang David.

Anyway, by the time we finished, David was trussed up from his feet to his chest. He looked like a jute bag with a head. But boy was he heavy — he must have weighed twice as much with all that rope. It took three of us to roll him over to the tree and lift him up on the branch.

But it still wasn't much fun because David still couldn't grasp the trouble he was in and kept smiling all the time. He stood on the branch and looked down at us and smiled. He was the center of attention at last and it pleased him, but the look on his face said that it confused him a bit too.

Then Stan put the noose over his head and pulled it down around his neck and tightened it and stepped back, a really solemn look on his face. I knew he'd seen that in the *Durango Kid* movie at the Opera House too. Taking a lead from Stan we all got solemn and subdued and quiet. In fact, we never got so far before, never actually hanged a captive and we were as absorbed, as fascinated by what we were about to do, as David was himself. But we weren't confused at all.

And then, just as Stan stepped forward to push David off the branch, just at the culmination of all our hard work, just when David was going to 'swing in the breeze' and 'dance on the air' (all expressions courtesy of the *Durango Kid* serial), all hell broke loose. My father used that expression on special occasions to describe an event that led, or could have led, to a fairly horrible and generally catastrophic end.

What we heard was a noise like thunder. A really angry, loud, booming thunder rolling down the hill. We froze. Had the Cowboys developed a new and terrifying weapon that none of us ever saw or heard before and were now employing it to wreak vengeance on us for hanging David?

Afterwards Jay Jay said he thought it might be the Devil. But it wasn't the Devil, it was something far worse. It was my Uncle Buster, Stan's father, 260 lbs of pure anger and fury barrelling towards us with the speed of a raging bull. I'd heard that expression in the same *Durango Kid* movie and now I knew what it really meant. I'd seen a raging bull once, in a field owned by an old Portuguese farmer down in Devonshire and it seemed tame in comparison to my uncle.

In one movement he scooped David off the branch and snatched the noose off his neck. By the time he set David on the ground and turned to face us Jay Jay and Jackie were halfway down the hill and disappearing fast. Stan and I just stood there rooted to the ground. We knew that running wasn't an option because we had to come home sometime and Uncle Buster would still be there. We also knew instinctively that our hanging days were over.

But at least one good thing happened that day. David didn't die. Not then.

We lived in a time when parents and relatives weren't intimidated by the thought of applying belts to bums of children who did wrong, and there was no doubt that we surely did wrong. For the next few days we ate standing up and slept on our stomachs.

The *Durango Kid* never hanged anybody in the movies. Now we knew why.

All the kids in the neighbourhood used to swim down at Forster's Bay because the Forster's house was on the North Shore and everybody who knew anything knew that the north side of the Island was the best side to swim on. The South Shore was no fun. It was just a whole lot of beaches, all sandy and flat and wavy and shallow, until you went out far enough to actually get in over your head.

Not to mention the tourists. They seemed to like it fine enough but then they really didn't know any better. It seemed that getting a tan, and getting it in a hurry, was one of the most important things they needed to do. Since most of them were really pale, pink and white we could understand why. We didn't have that problem and we were more than willing to leave that side of the Island to them. We had rocks to jump off, deep water to dive into and no sand in our trunks to stick to our willies.

The Forsters built their house at the top of a pretty high cliff, so to get down to the water to swim you had to climb down a narrow, rough and steep path. But it was worth it. Where we swam the water at high tide was about twenty feet deep and almost eighteen at low tide because there isn't much of a tidal range in Bermuda. It was so deep that none of us kids could dive to the bottom, although it was sometimes a challenge to try.

My mom said that's where I damaged my ear, trying to dive to the bottom of Forster's Bay, but actually that happened one time when we were playing enemy soldiers and Jackie hit me up side my head in a moment of feverish excitement which Jay Jay said was brought on by bloodlust. None of us really understood what that meant but Jay Jay said he read it in one of his comic books. It sounded really cool, so even though I couldn't hear anything out of that ear for two days it was worth it because now I was important — I was hit by bloodlust.

Nobody wanted to try to dive to the bottom that particular day, so we figured we'd all jump in and make the water boil. To do that we formed a rough circle in the water and at the word "Go" we'd all start to kick our feet and pound our fists as fast and as hard as we could until the water surface was just a layer of bubbling white foam.

But when you made the water boil you couldn't see anything below the surface so we couldn't see

David lying on the bottom twenty feet under us. He was there because he was David and David always wanted to be part of everything we other kids did. Even though he was the smallest. Even though we hanged him. Even though he couldn't swim. But he always had an inflated car inner tube to keep him afloat, and it wasn't until we stopped making the water boil that we saw the inner tube floating away toward Dockyard, round and black and empty.

His mother was the one who came. The memory of her coming is as alive in me today as it was then, so long ago. She came in her housecoat, thin and white because it was summer. It flowed behind her like a cape as she sprinted across Forster's lawn and without breaking stride leapt from the highest cliff overlooking that deep and almost empty embayment.

She flew, the coat open and streaming behind her like wings, and when she entered it the water seemed to part for her and she swept to the bottom in an instant. She surfaced with David in her arms, dashed up the path to the top of the cliff and was gone.

He lay in his bedroom, dressed in a brown suit and a tie with little yellow horses running over it. I'd never seen him in anything other than shorts and T-shirts before so at first I didn't recognize him. His hair was also combed and brushed, which didn't make it any easier. He was quiet and his eyes were closed and he was still and straight and faintly blue and on his lips was the smallest of smiles.

I stayed with him for a long while and didn't leave until my mom came to take me away. She said afterwards that I said he spoke to me, and she waited for me to answer. I told her what he said. He said "I bet the *Durango Kid* never drowned anybody either." She looked at me in a curious, different way, half smiled, patted me gently on the head, and we left.

David's funeral was the next day. He was already dead when his mother took him from the waters of Forster's Bay.

Chapter 2
Long Leroy

Everybody talked really quietly, walked around with sad looks on their faces and sighed and shook their heads with no smiles at all. Everybody but me. I was super-excited because this was going to be my first funeral ever and my best friend David was going to be the star. This was even better than the *Durango Kid* serial at Opera House on Saturday afternoons.

My dad told me that David would be in a coffin, which he said was like a big, long box with fancy decorations and metal handles on the side for people to carry it around. David would be lying in it and he'd be dressed up even better than he'd been in his bedroom yesterday and people would come and look at him and say nice things about him, even people who didn't know him. He'd be the center of attention, just like he always wanted to be. Boy, he was really going to like that. My mom got hold of me and held my hands and said I needed to settle down and probably wipe the smile off my face because people didn't act like that at funerals, especially if their best friend was the one who was dead.

I tried to explain to her that David wasn't really dead because he spoke to me when he lay in his bed after his mom saved him from drowning.

But my mom sighed and wiped her eyes and said that she hadn't really saved him and that I probably just imagined that he spoke to me because he was dead when I saw him in his bedroom. I tried again to tell her that if he was dead he couldn't have talked to me because everybody knew that dead people didn't do that sort of thing. My mom nodded her head really slowly and agreed that as far as she knew, dead people didn't. Then she looked at my face and she looked at my dad and she got up and said we'd just leave it at that for now.

For the funeral my mom got out my best khaki shorts, the ones with the turned up cuffs, and a clean white shirt and my one bow tie. On the whole I was really a lucky kid. I lived in the best place in the world with the best family you could have so I generally liked everything in my life, except for two things which I really hated. One of the two things I really hated was to have anything tied around my neck, so my mom bought me just one bow tie. She probably figured that if I had two I might think I'd have to wear them twice as often and she wasn't ready for the trouble that could cause.

The other thing I really hated was getting my picture taken, and it seemed that those two things always happened at the same time. Whenever I wore my bow tie I looked 'just like a real little man, so nice and clean' like my mom always said. It was true, because every time I was forced to wear a tie the occasion was always so important I had to get a bath first, even if it wasn't Saturday night. Then my mom would decide she just had to get a picture of me.

So I'd stand like a statue with a really nasty pout on my face while my dad took pictures. The nasty pout was my revenge. Nothing could make me smile for a picture-taking torture session. Not threats, not pleas, not promises of Simmons pineapple sherbet, which everyone knew was the best on the whole island.

What used to bother my mom most was that when she showed people pictures of me, like a lot of moms do to show off their kids, she spent a lot of time explaining that in spite of what the pictures looked like I really wasn't a rotten kid, it was just a phase I was going through that I'd eventually grow out of.

Anyway, my dad took pictures and we got in our car and left for the church. But by this time I was really mad at David because if it wasn't for him I wouldn't have had to wear that stupid bow tie and get my stupid picture taken. But by the time we got to the church and I went inside and saw the box he was in up at the front and his mom and dad and his two older brothers crying and blowing their noses into tissues that were soggy and limp I wasn't mad any more.

But I was sort of disappointed because the whole funeral service inside the church was like a brownish blur to me. Not because it all happened so fast or anything like that, but because Mrs. Hunt was sitting in the pew directly in front of me and Mrs. Hunt was about six feet tall and really fat and she wore a brown dress and a brown jacket and all I saw the whole time was Mrs. Hunt's big, brown back.

Then we went outside and my dad took my hand and we walked up between the graves and I could see a lot better. But I wished I couldn't because everyone stopped beside one grave that was opened up, and I thought about skeletons and dead things in that deep, dark hole and I realized that this was where they were going to put David. And I knew then that my mom was right — David was really dead.

All the kids from the Hill were there and nobody said anything about my khaki shorts and my white shirt and my bow tie because we all had on khaki shorts and white shirts and bow ties. We looked like we'd all been dressed by the same mom. David's mom cried some more and then the minister took her by the arm and led her back down through the graves and we all followed behind them. When we got to the church gate we kids all got together and for a while no one said anything because we weren't sure what we should actually say in a situation like this, mainly because none of us had ever been in a situation like this. Then Jay Jay said "Hey, remember the time we almost hanged him?" and that got us all laughing at the thought of David tied up like a mummy. He would have laughed too. Then we agreed that once we got home and into some decent clothes we'd all meet out back of my house and spend the afternoon playing Cowboys and Indians.

But there was a problem — who'd we get to replace David? We were always really careful to make sure there was the same number of Cowboys as Indians, otherwise there were always arguments about one side having more Cowboys than the other side had Indians or the other way around. Now with David being dead and everything we needed someone to take his place, even if only to avoid those arguments. But we had to be really careful about who we chose because he had to be someone who really fit into our Hill Gang, someone we could trust to uphold all our values and keep our secrets even under the worst enemy torture. Secrets like where our forts were and where to find the best floppers.

And now you're probably wondering: 'What are floppers'? Well, floppers were one of the most important plants on the whole island. They were known and loved by every kid on the Hill and every other kid who lived and played anywhere near any wooded or wilderness area in Bermuda. They were only about two or three feet tall and they had these really wonderful, amazing things — they had leaves. Okay, so you're thinking that every plant has leaves and that may be true, but every plant didn't have flopper leaves, leaves that were smooth and soft and round and about the size of a grownup's hand. Leaves that were right there when we kids — who'd spent hours building forts and secret hideouts, playing Cowboys and Indians and African hunters, eating food and lemonade we'd taken from home — needed to go to the bathroom.

Number One was okay, we could pee anywhere, but Number Two could have been a real problem. See, even though we had forts and secret hideouts and stuff none of them had toilets, and who wanted to go all the way back home just to have a poop? And sometimes we had to poop right away, especially if we ate anything that Jay Jay made.

But when we had to go we just picked out one of our special places, pulled down our pants and went, and when we finished we'd reach out and grab a couple of leaves off the flopper plant right in front of us and wipe our bums. They were smooth as toilet paper and always cool. Stan said it was actually better than toilet paper because you were using nature and giving back to her all at the same time.

Stan was really smart and thought about things like that.

So that's what you need to know about floppers.

Anyway, we had to make a decision and everyone had to agree — who were we going to choose to be the newest member of our gang?

It was Jackie who first suggested him, in a really quiet voice. "Leroy', he said, "Long Leroy."

Nobody said anything for a while; we had to think about that one. Finally Stan said, "All right, let's take a vote. Hands up for inviting Long Leroy."

Everybody's hand went up, everybody's except Jay Jay's.

"I'm in a state of flux," he said, and we all stared at him.

"Jay Jay's got a new expression," Stan said, and we all nodded. Every now and then Jay Jay would come up with a word or an expression, usually one he got from his latest comic book, and try it out on us. Usually nobody but Stan knew what it meant, not even Jay Jay. We all looked at Stan expectantly. "It means he's got a problem with Leroy."

Jay Jay shook his head. "It's not really a problem with Leroy, well, not with all of him, just, uh, just with part of him."

We stared at Jay Jay some more but we were pretty sure we knew what part of Leroy was bothering him.

Okay, I told you about floppers, now I have to tell you about Leroy. We called him Shy Leroy at first because he was always kind of quiet and kind of private too, but that all changed after The Incident.

We had the first car on the Hill, a Ford Prefect made somewhere in England. It was black — not shiny black, not brilliant-and-bright-in-the Bermuda-sun black, not see-your-face-like-in-a-mirror black, but dull black, boring black, black with brush streaks running in all different directions because it had been painted by Mr. Outerbridge who lived in St. Georges. Mr. Outerbridge bought the car second hand when it was eight years old and had a few rust spots on it. He decided that the best thing to do would be to paint over them. The car was a pale, creamy white when he bought it but he had three gallons of flat black paint in his shed and figured it would be cheaper just to use that. Besides, he thought black would be a better colour anyway because then any future rust spots wouldn't show up as easily.

My dad said he was a cheap blad of a bull, which was one of my dad's favourite expressions. He didn't curse like ordinary people; he just used phrases like that but they had the same impact as the worst curses I ever heard, just by the way he said them. I asked him once what 'blad of a bull' meant and he said it was a St. David's Island curse and it meant 'bladder of a bull'. I said "Oh," and left it at that. I

31

didn't know what 'bladder of a bull' meant either but if it came from St. David's Island it had to be bad.

The Ford Prefect was okay if you were driving on the flat, but we lived right at the top of the Hill and the Hill was steep and the car didn't have much power. So to get home anyone who was in it except my mom had to get out and walk up the Hill. When she was ready my mom would gun the engine, floor the gas pedal and begin her run. The engine would make a noise like my granny's sewing machine and the car would lurch across the road and start up the Hill. Smoke would stream from the exhaust pipe and sometimes from some place under the hood. Mom's face was pretty scary at those times because her lips would be pressed tight and her nostrils would be moving in and out and sometimes you could see sweat on her forehead. Sometimes, if we had something heavy like packages or groceries in the car, we'd have to get behind and push and slowly, very slowly the Prefect would climb up the Hill to our house.

In spite of the fact that it was old and rusty and had no power there was one really wonderful thing about the Ford Prefect that made it truly beautiful in the eyes of us kids. It had a hole in the floor. But this was no ordinary hole, not a hole that came from rust and deterioration because of age, humidity and salt sea air. No, this was a genuine, deliberate, perfectly round, man-made, carefully cut out opening in the floor just in front of the rear seats in the back of the car.

Stan discovered it, of course. He made all the important discoveries and this was definitely one of the best. What happened was one afternoon he dropped a penny on the car floor and while he was looking for it he noticed a little wire loop on the carpet so he tugged on it and came up with a piece of the carpet and there it was — the hole. It was as round as one of my mom's pancakes and you could look through it and see the ground underneath. We figured it must have been put there to help clean up the floor — you pulled out the plug and swept any dirt out through the hole.

That might have been what it was meant for by the people who made the car but for us it had an entirely different use. For us it was a pee hole. We could lift up the plug, take out our willies, aim through the hole and squirt. Nothing was more exciting than travelling along those narrow Bermuda roads watching your pee hitting the asphalt in a hissing splash and disappearing behind you at fifteen miles an hour.

My mom never caught on, at least not until The Incident, even though she had plenty of opportunities because we had a lot of narrow escapes. One of her earliest clues should have been what stopped happening when we were taking really long drives like the one from our house to St. Georges, which was twelve miles away at the eastern end of the island. What stopped happening was our usual nagging to pull the car over so we could get out and go pee in the bushes on the side of the road. Not that we really ever needed to go, it was just fun to pee in the bushes. But the nagging abruptly stopped. That should have been a dead giveaway.

We spread the word, of course, and all the boys on the Hill wanted to try it. So we always tried to arrange to have at least one or two of them go with us in the back seat if we were driving any distance, like into town or up to Pontoons in Spanish Point for a swim. We charged them a penny to pee in the hole. It was turning out to be a really good business, although my mom couldn't understand why it was that whenever she drove up the Hill to our house all the kids around would start shouting "Penny a pee! Penny a pee!" That should have been a bit of a clue too, but mom just put it down to kids being kids. Rude kids, sure, but kids none the less.

The girls eventually heard about the pee hole. We think it was Jay Jay who told them because he'd been hinting that it'd be fun to see if a girl could aim as good as a boy. Stan was the only one of us who showed any real interest in Jay Jay's idea. He figured that given the right circumstances, meaning a combination of flat road, slow speed and proper positioning, a girl would probably be just as accurate as any of us boys. Jay Jay was convinced that no girl could be as good, mainly because a girl didn't have anything she could hold onto and aim.

Stan still insisted that proper positioning was the key and that girls learned how to do this from the time they got out of diapers. But Jay Jay wouldn't back down and he even bet Stan two comic books that none of the girls on the Hill could aim well enough to pee through the hole. But in the end it didn't matter because none of the girls was interested in trying and at that stage in our lives none of us really cared. Except maybe Stan, but he was older than most of us and seemed to think we'd missed a good opportunity. We weren't too sure what the opportunity actually was that we'd missed, but in any case the rest of us felt the pee hole was a boy thing and we were happy to keep it that way.

Bermudians are friendly, sociable and generally willing to lend a hand to anyone in trouble, even to anyone they think might not be in trouble yet but could be heading into it, and it was this attitude that almost gave the pee hole away. One time we were driving up in Paget with Jay Jay, Jackie and me in the back when we decided to put the pee hole to use. All of a sudden we heard a horn beeping behind us and when we looked out the back window we saw a man in a car waving his hand up and down and shouting something that none of us could hear.

My mom tended to ignore people who drove like that, assuming that they wanted to pass and were rudely demonstrating their intent. When that happened she'd speed up so the person couldn't pass. It was her way of reacting to what she considered to be a case of very bad manners, no doubt relating back to inadequate parenting on both the mother's and father's side, and if ignoring the insistent beeping and frantic waving of the arms of the ill-bred person behind her would somehow teach that person a long overdue lesson in polite road behaviour, she was quite willing to do so.

But after another careful look in the rear view mirror to see if the driver had learned his lesson she recognized him — Mr. Simons, a friend of my dad — and decided to pull over to let him pass. As soon as she did Mr. Simons swerved to a stop behind us, got out of his car and ran to mom's window.

"Mrs. D, Mrs. D, please turn off your ignition key immediately! Your radiator's leaking and you're in danger of ruining your engine. I've been beeping and waving trying to get your attention. Didn't you see me?"

Sometimes kids can be a real asset for parents who find themselves in situations that might be troublesome from a social point of view. My mom looked Mr. Simons right in the eyes and shook her head. "It's these children," she said, "they make so much noise that sometimes you can't hear a thing, and only one of them is really quiet when you tell him to be. Mine. The others are friends of his. They don't listen." She shook her head again. The implication was obvious — bad parenting on the part of all the other moms and dads. I looked at Jay Jay and Jackie and we all hung our heads. None of us had been making a sound but we knew our roles and we were happy to play along and help my mom out.

Mr. Simons nodded in complete understanding, cast a stern look at us in the back seat, walked around to the front of the car, opened the hood and poked around inside. We were all very quiet because we had an idea where this might lead, and where that might be wasn't going to be good for the future of the pee hole. Mr. Simons poked around some more, pulled his head from under the hood, stood up and shrugged.

"The radiator looks good, it doesn't appear to be leaking at all." Then he saw the expression on my mom's face, which said pretty loud and clear that she was not happy with the prognosis, the diagnosis or the result of the investigation. Mr. Simons tried to explain that he'd seen, as he put it, "a sudden burst of water coming from under the car." Mom got out of the car, walked deliberately to the back, stopped for a few seconds then returned to the driver's door, where Mr. Simons stood looking very sheepish.

She spoke to him in the soft tone of voice that all parents seem to possess when something really bad is about to happen to their children. Something bad delivered by the parents themselves. We sat like statues in the back seat, not daring to utter a word. Was it possible that mom was actually going to spank Mr. Simons? Her tone of voice made it seem like a real possibility. But Mr. Simons got off easily. Mom merely thanked him quietly for his concern, got back into the car, wound up her window and uttered a single sentence. In the back seat we all assumed looks as serious as mom's to show our complete agreement with her assessment of Mr. Simons, whom she deemed in no uncertain terms to be "a bloody, blind, bladder of a bull."

But it wasn't Mr. Simons who caused the downfall of the Penny-a-Pee business, it was Shy Leroy and The Incident. It happened the day that me, Stan, Jay Jay, and Leroy were in the back seat on a drive up to Warwick. When it came his turn Shy Leroy didn't want any of us to see his privates so he decided to lie down on the floor right over the hole and do his business. Now this was strictly against procedure, which all of us knew was that you kneeled down just above the pee-hole and you aimed. But we bent the rules for Leroy 'cause he was so shy and it would have worked too, except for two things. One was Leroy sticking his willie right down through the hole. The other was the broken cedar branch in the middle of the road that my mom tried to avoid hitting but didn't turn soon enough and ran right over.

Both things happened at about the same time, resulting in a really terrible scream by Shy Leroy, the near ditching of the car by my mom, and gasps of awe and admiration by us kids at what Leroy was clutching in his hands. It's true we'd heard talk about it before, rumours and stuff from some of the kids who lived down below the Hill, but we knew you can't always trust rumours, especially from kids down below the Hill. But boy, this was even better than any of the rumours we'd heard.

I mean, it was amazing because even with both his hands around it part of it was still sticking out, and Leroy had big hands. It was definitely a case of the real thing living up to and beyond any of our expectations. I think mom was as impressed as we were when she turned around and saw what Leroy was holding because there was the same look on her face as she had the time my Uncle Buster brought home the biggest lobster any of us ever saw.

But then she stopped looking and shook her head like she was trying to clear away the image of what she'd seen, and we knew right away that we were in trouble. After some loud, pointed and really aggressive questions, with a lot of arm waving, finger pointing and some serious threats, the whole story came out.

That night in the shed out back of the house my dad was called into action and a drastic change took place in our car as the lid on the pee-hole was glued shut forever. And there was one other thing that changed too — Leroy's nickname. We never called him 'Shy' again, he was 'Long Leroy' from that day on.

Anyway, that'll tell you something about Leroy and maybe give you an idea about the part of Leroy that was causing Jay Jay's state of flux.

"See," Jay Jay said, "Leroy could really mess us up. Kids talk, right, and by now I bet almost every kid in Pembroke has heard about Leroy's willie. So anytime we have a war with any gang that's not from the Hill they're all going to try to capture Leroy. Hey, if we were them that's what we'd do. And when they do they'll try to show off his thing and what's more, they'll probably charge kids to see it."

This was serious stuff, really serious stuff, stuff we never considered but Jay Jay did. He had a really devious mind. It was Stan who came up with the solution. He figured that maybe before we made any big decisions we should talk to Leroy, tell him we were thinking about asking him to join our gang and let him know right up front the dangers he could possibly face. So we waited for Leroy and met up with him as he was leaving church and asked him to meet us later in my back yard.

That afternoon we all stood around while Stan explained the situation to Leroy. He seemed kind of disinterested in the whole idea and we could see that we really didn't have his full attention, at least not until Stan mentioned the part about the other guys charging to see his willie. Then he seemed to perk right up and we knew that we just might be looking at our next Hill Gang member. When he finished explaining Stan asked him if he had any questions.

"Yeah," Leroy said, "just one. How much do you figure they'd charge?"

In the end Leroy decided not to join us and two days later we heard he'd started a business in an old shed in the bushes out behind his house. Inside he was charging customers to see his willie — thruppence for a five second viewing. For sixpence you got ten seconds, plus you could touch it to make sure it was real.

Chapter 3
Pimps

Every kid on the Hill knew about Leroy Davis' new business. Every kid on the Hill knew that Leroy was making a lot of money. And every kid on the Hill knew that the best part of it, at least for Leroy, was that all he had to do was just stand there and pull down his shorts and the thruppences, and sometimes even the sixpences, just rolled in. What could be better than that?

So of course problems arose as soon as word about his business left the Hill and got into the other neighborhoods. When kids in the other gangs in the Parish heard about the money Leroy was making they decided to set up businesses of their own. But they had one big problem — they didn't have Leroy. We didn't either, but we were going to get him, and in the end getting him was pretty easy.

It all started because the roof on Leroy's house leaked. It had been leaking for a long time and his mom always solved the problem with pots and pans. She used to put them under the leaks and it worked, at least for a while. But then a really bad storm hit with days and days of rain — tank rain.

Okay, I'm going to have to tell you about tank rain. See, my dad told me that in almost every country in the world people got their fresh water from lakes or rivers or streams. But we don't have any lakes or rivers or streams in Bermuda. Not one lake, not one river, not one stream. What we do have is rain. That's where we get our fresh water. Rain falls on our roofs and we collect it.

The roofs on Bermuda houses are different from roofs anywhere else in the world. They're all really white and they're all really white for a reason. They're made out of limestone slates about an inch thick and maybe a foot square. The slates are cut from big blocks in limestone quarries and they're laid down on a cedar wood frame on the roof. When the roof is completely covered the slates are plastered with cement wash and then painted with white lime wash. Not only does this make our roofs really, really white, it also cleans up the rain water that falls on the roofs. At the edges of the roofs there are gutters and at the end of the gutters there are pipes that lead down into tanks. So, rain falls on the roofs, flows to the gutters, runs down the pipes and into the tanks.

So now I'm going to have to tell you about tanks. Under our houses we don't have cellars or basements or storerooms. We have tanks. Really big tanks. The sides and bottoms of our tanks are built of limestone blocks covered with cement, and the tank under our house is about two feet taller than my dad and as wide and as long as our kitchen and dining room together. My dad calls it a mini-sized swimming pool, except you can't swim in it because it's covered over with really big slabs of concrete about a foot thick. It has to be covered pretty good because if not the weight of the house on top of it could make it collapse, and that wouldn't be good. But as far as I know, nobody has ever drowned from falling into a tank under their house. In fact, as far as I know nobody has ever fallen into a tank even without drowning.

Of course, every tank has a trap door or something like that where you can look down and check it out to see if everything is all right with it, and sometimes you have to check it out because it might develop a leak or something. Then you have to drain it and get down into it and fix the leak, and that was a 'Godalmighty, blad-of-a-bull pain in the arse,' so my dad said.

So if you're really hung up on cellars or basements or storerooms and you're thinking along those lines then it might be easier to think of a big, one room basement or cellar with no windows and no doors. Then think of the basement or cellar being filled with the freshest, sweetest-tasting water you could ever imagine, and there you have it — a Bermuda tank. We pump the water from the tank to use in our houses and it comes out of taps just like anywhere else in the world. Sometimes tourists have a hard time figuring out the tank system, which was funny because it's pretty simple if you think about it. But as my dad said, most tourists don't come to Bermuda to think.

So, we depended on rain to fill our tanks. But sometimes it didn't rain for weeks, well, not really good rain anyway, maybe we'd just have a shower or two that lasted only five or ten minutes, or even worse, maybe it would just sprinkle. When it didn't rain the water level in our tank would get lower and lower and my dad would open the trap door every day and you could almost tell the level of the water by the number of swear words he used to describe what he saw. My mom would try to shush him if we kids were nearby but we stuck around to listen because my dad always came up with new and really good words that we could use when we were mad at members of other gangs, and sometimes at each other.

But sometimes when it rained it really rained hard and it would rain for a long time and if you went out in it you'd get soaked in a second. When it rained like that the water would gush into our tank with such force you could hear it if you were in the kitchen up above. And in times of drought when it hadn't rained for weeks this is what Bermudians needed and loved — rain so hard and long it filled the empty and nearly empty tanks — tank rain.

And that's what we got when the storm hit. Four straight days of rain, rain that pounded down on every roof in Bermuda, including the roof on Leroy's house. And Leroy's mom didn't have nearly enough pots and pans to put under every leak in her house. So in the middle of emptying the old chamber pot her mother left her that she used because she'd run out of pots and pans she made Mr. Davis promise to finally fix the roof or else. And it was a well-known fact around the Hill that Mr. Davis, who was about half the size of Mrs. Davis, was no match for her in any fight of any kind, and if she said 'or else' Mr. Davis knew that he'd be in real trouble if he didn't do his best to make sure that 'or else' never happened.

So he got his friend Micey Ming to deliver a load of limestone roof slates in his old, beat-up truck so he could start work on the roof as soon as possible and therefore avoid the 'or else' that Mrs. Davis promised. Of course all of us in the Hill Gang went down to watch them unload the slates off the truck because we liked to see other people work. We didn't help because the slates were too heavy for us kids to lift, except for Stan, who was big enough but wasn't interested in doing donkey work, as he put it.

We all thought they'd put the slates in Leroy's back yard, but Micey had loaded enough slate to repair the roof on the old shed too, the one that

Leroy was using for his business. Micey said it would make things a lot easier if they just put the slate inside the shed and Mr. Davis said that was a good idea, but first he had to go down and move a few things around to make room for the slates. So that's what he did.

None of us kids knew that's what he planned to do and neither did Leroy. But none of us kids was inside the shed with our shorts down around our ankles and Annie Bascombe in front of us looking at our willie and going "oh my, oh my!' But Leroy was. He had a smile on his face and sixpence in his hand and Annie was just reaching out to get her money's worth when his dad pulled the shed door wide open. We knew that when the shed door was shut Leroy was probably inside going about his business so we were kind of prepared to see what was going on. Mr. Davis wasn't.

What happened next happened so fast it's still kind of a blur in my mind. I remember a flash of yellow and red streaking out the door and disappearing round the corner of the shed. That was Annie in her red and yellow dress that she only wore on special occasions, like birthdays and church. I guess she figured the visit to Leroy was a special occasion too. We didn't see Annie for a long time after that, and she never did come back to claim the thruppence Leroy owed her for not getting the full sixpence deal.

Mr. Davis stood by the door while Leroy pulled up his shorts as fast as he could and we stood there too, just as still and quiet as we could be waiting for disaster to strike. Of course we didn't run away or anything like that because we needed to see the punishment, the terrible punishment that was going to come. After all, we were kids and kids kind of like terrible punishment, as long as it's happening to someone else. But nothing happened right away so I guessed Mr. Davis was struck dumb by what he saw. I snuck a look up at him and I was almost struck dumb by what I saw. Mr. Davis was smiling. Actually, Mr. Davis was grinning, as big a grin as I'd ever seen on his face. And then finally he said something, something none of us ever expected to hear. He said, "That's my boy." And we all started grinning too.

But Leroy wasn't too happy because with all the slates filling up the shed there was no place in his yard to run his business and he knew he'd have to close it down. We all kind of acted like we felt sorry for him but we really didn't. After all, we'd asked him to become a member of the Hill Gang, but he didn't want to; he was more interested in making money.

"Serves him right," Jackie said. "He should have joined the Gang when we gave him the chance, then at least he'd have been one of us."

We headed back up the Hill, giggling and laughing, feeling pretty good because of what happened to Leroy. No business, no money, no Gang. And best of all, it didn't matter now if he had the biggest willie on the Hill.

Then Jay Jay stopped in mid giggle. "We're stupid," he said, 'we're so stupid."

Stan looked at him and scowled. "We're what?"

"Stupid," Jay Jay repeated. Then he saw the look on Stan's face. Stan hated to be called 'stupid'.

"Not you," Jay Jay said," not you. It's the rest of us, we're stupid. We're looking a gift horse in the mouth."

"A what horse in the what?"

"It's got to be from one of his comic books," I said.

Jay Jay nodded. "It was in one of my *Illustrated Comic Classics*. What it means is we're gonna make some money, and we're gonna do it off Leroy's willie!"

"We already tried. He doesn't want to join the Gang."

"Doesn't have to, I got a plan."

Stan snorted. "Is this your normal-type plan or is this a sensible one, which would be really different."

'It's a good, sensible plan, a great plan, and I've got one word for it, 'rental property.'"

"That's two words, Jay Jay, and they both sound stupid."

Jay Jay sighed. "Okay, here's what we do. We offer to rent a place to Leroy where he can do his business. It'll be safe and secure because we'll protect it, and we'll charge him a penny for every thrupenny look and tuppence for every sixpenny feel!"

Stan looked at Jay Jay like he was seeing him for the first time, then he nodded his head and we knew that he liked what he heard.

"That's a pretty good plan, Jay Jay."

"Yeah, Jay Jay," the rest of us joined in, nodding our heads too. 'That's a pretty good plan."

"But where's the place going to be?" I was a little concerned because none of our yards had a spare shed, and those that we did have were too close to our houses and we all knew it was much too risky for Leroy to do his business anywhere near our moms and dads. If they saw what Mr. Davis witnessed they sure wouldn't have the same reaction he did. There wouldn't have been any grinning or smiling or 'That's my boy' stuff. Punishment would have been swift and terrible and the worst part is that we'd have gotten the same as Leroy, probably more.

Jay Jay smiled, enjoying the fact that all of us were waiting for him to deliver the answer. Generally when he was the center of attention it was because he'd messed up somehow and gotten us all into trouble. But we knew that this time was different because he was smiling and didn't look like he was ready to duck and run before Stan could smack him up side his head for messing up again.

"Okay," he said, and his voice rose up and he stood right at attention, like the minister always did in church before he delivered the final sentence in his sermon, "the place is going to be the Oleander Fort."

Stan was the one who took the proposal to Leroy, and in two days he moved his business into the Fort. Jay Jay took on the job of Business Manager and just inside the door he stood a wooden mango box on its side to use as a desk. He sat on a tree stump behind it and collected money in two empty Condensed Milk cans, one for thruppences, the other for sixpennies. At the end of the day he divided up the money and everybody was happy. For a while.

When the end came it came suddenly and swiftly.

About two weeks after we set up in the Oleander Fort I sat in the kitchen looking at the comics from the weekend edition of the *Mid Ocean News* while my dad went through the rest of the newspaper. Then he started to laugh and my mom asked him what was so funny.

"They finally got Slimey Limey."

"Who's Slimey Limey?" was my first question, 'cause I usually had at least two more depending on the situation.

"Slimey', my dad said, "is a man who came here from England about a hundred years ago and has been engaged in some pretty dodgy activities since that time."

"A hundred years?"

"Okay, maybe a little less, it just seems like a hundred to most people who know about him."

"So who got him?"

"The police. They arrested him for pimping those two ladies of his."

My mom's eyebrows shot up and her face looked like she'd swallowed a fart.

"Hmmph, it's about time they finally got a hold of Slimey because he's been getting away with being a pimp for way too long. And incidentally," she said, firing kind of a mean look at my dad, "there is absolutely nothing lady-like about those two ladies." Then she called them something else that didn't sound too good just by the way she said it. Of course I was interested in what they were talking about, especially the pimping part, which sounded really bad. It must be if you got arrested for it.

"What's a pimp?" I mean, I had to ask because that's what the conversation was all about. My mom threw one of those looks at my dad that said 'You better watch what you say because that boy will repeat every word.'

My dad sort of took his time to answer, and he looked at my mom and she said "Careful," and he shook his head and sighed. "Well, a pimp is a person who helps a lady to sell sex." Then he added real quickly, "But it's a really bad thing to do and you can get arrested by the police for doing it, just like Slimey, and you can also go to jail."

"What does that mean, selling sex? Is it like in a shop or something, like cigarettes or rum, something that's bad for your health?"

My mom snorted and said, "That's debatable," and my dad said, "It means paying someone so you can, ahhh, so you can touch their private parts, and a pimp is the one who arranges everything and shares the money."

Later when I told Stan he said "Oh shit" real quietly and we realized that for two weeks we had all been pimps and that unless we acted quickly, in a little while we could all be in jail.

I got all the Gang together as fast as I could. Jay Jay came running up the Hill with Jackie and Arnold right behind him. Well, Jackie was right behind him but because of the fact that he was really fat and couldn't run very fast Arnold was actually way behind him. He managed to catch up in the time it took for Jay Jay and Jackie to meet up with Stan and me at the top of the Hill.

Arnold's house was at the very bottom of the Hill, so although he didn't really live on the Hill he always wanted to be a member of our Hill Gang. We finally gave in and put him through a three month trial period to make sure he could withstand all the hardships endured by a true Gang member. Although he failed a couple of our toughest fitness tests we still welcomed him into the Gang. The fact that his mom made the best taffy candy and coconut cakes in Pembroke Parish was the deciding factor in his favour.

Jay Jay was trying to catch his breath and talk at the same time, so his question came out in a whisper "Okay, so what's up?"

"We got to have an Emergency Council meeting and we got to have it right now," I said, "because we could be in really big trouble."

Nobody called an Emergency Council meeting unless something really important was happening or about to happen, like an attack by another neighbourhood gang, armed with sling shots and homemade bows and arrows and maybe even spitballs trying to take over one of our Forts, at least until they all had to go back home for lunch or supper. We had to tell Leroy right away, so Jay Jay went down to his house to get him so we could all be together when we broke the bad news. Anyway, it didn't take us long to get down to the Fort and we were lucky because it was Leroy's day off so we had it to ourselves.

Leroy took it much better than we thought he would and when we asked him why he wasn't mad or scared or even really bothered about shutting down the business he said he was getting a little worried about it anyway, especially about the touching part. See, his willie had gotten so famous even some of the bigger girls were coming to the Fort, not just to look at it but to touch it too.

'Sometimes they do more than just touch it" Leroy said. "Sometimes they grab on to it too, and that's what bothers me."

"Oh yeah," Jay Jay said, "Hey, a grab is obviously worth more money than a touch and those girls were getting away without paying anything extra. That's practically stealing."

Leroy shook his head. "That's not it. I think that all that grabbing might be bad for me, bad for my willie."

"Were they hurting it?" I was kind of curious, even though when I compared my willie to Leroy's I knew I'd never have to worry about any girls wanting to grab it.

"Well, they weren't really hurting it — actually it felt kind of …umm… never mind. No, the thing was that after some of them grabbed me it used to swell up a bit and I figure that if it ever swelled up too much and stayed like that I'd have a lot of trouble peeing."

This kind of problem was something that none of us had ever experienced, but since peeing was a really important part of our regular day to day lives, not to mention a lot of our competitions, we could understand Leroy's concern.

Since he didn't have his business anymore and we still needed another member to fill David's place we asked Leroy once again to join the Hill Gang, and once again he refused. He said he had his reputation to think about, and he didn't want to be associated with a gang whose members were all potential jail birds.

Chapter 4
The Opera House

Saturday was the most wonderful day of the week for all the kids on the Hill and most of the other kids in Pembroke Parish. Not so much because you didn't have to go to school, although that counted for a whole lot; not so much because Saturday was hot dog or hamburger for supper day, although that was pretty cool too, and not so much because you got your allowance on Saturday, although that gave you the opportunity to do what made Saturday the most wonderful day of the week. And that was to go to the movies at Opera House down Victoria Road in Hamilton.

The Durango Kid serial used to play at Opera House every Saturday. Well, every Saturday when they weren't playing a serial with Gene Autry or Roy Rogers, who only *thought* that he was King of the Cowboys. We didn't like Gene Autry or Roy Rogers because their outfits were boring and their horses were brown. They wore clothes that didn't match, like checked shirts and tan pants and white hats, and worst of all — every now and then, for no reason whatsoever, they sang a song. What was there to like about any of that?

But the *Durango Kid* was different. His shirt was black and he wore black pants, black boots and a black Stetson hat. His mask covered his eyes, with slits for him to see through, and it was black too. To make things even better — his horse was white. Pure white from head to hoof, so sometimes if the lighting and the background was just right the Durango Kid looked like he was riding on air. Gene Autry and Roy Rogers didn't stand a chance. We all tried to be like the *Durango Kid* but we all fell short. Nobody could really be like him, nobody could match his awesomeness.

Nobody — except Rickie Ratteray.

Rickie Ratteray. We spoke his name in hushed voices. Whispered it as if speaking it in normal tones would somehow tarnish his image, make him less of a fantasy and more real, more kidlike than godlike.

The thing about Rickie was that his cowboy outfit was complete. Totally. The thing about his cowboy outfit was that it was black. Totally. Black boots, black pants, black shirt, black vest, black Stetson hat. He looked like Son of the Durango Kid, except for the horse. Rickie was awesome. Not awesome like just really cool, he was awesome in the true sense of the word. When he walked up the street to Opera House he literally struck awe into all of us kids. There were even stirrups on his boots, black of course, so that when he walked he clinked, just like a real cowboy.

But the thing that was the absolute best, the thing that really put Rickie on a different astral plane was his gun belt and what it held, because what it held were two big, black, beautiful Colt revolvers. And that wasn't all, because the belt had special holsters and when the guns were in them the handles were reversed. Reversed. Gene Autry and Roy Rogers didn't even have two guns, much less ones with the handles reversed.

And Rickie's two-handed crossover draw was a wonder to behold. He could whip out those guns in the blink of an eye and if you worked up enough courage to challenge him he'd draw, shoot and holster those black beauties before you'd cleared your weapon. We'd draw straws to pick a challenger just to see him in action and the loser got to be the victim. Nobody outdrew Rickie, not even Stan. They said Rickie practiced for an hour every day after school and even more on the weekends. He went through a lot of caps in the run of a week.

Another thing about Rickie was he never stood in line. No matter what time he got to Opera House or how many people were there already he always went right to the front. And nobody got upset, nobody said a thing. That was his due — he had the outfit and he had the guns. In our priority system he'd earned the right to be first in line.

When we got to the ticket booth we'd pay the one shilling ticket price and head for the candy bar. Of course it sold more than candy but to us it was the candy bar. For sixpence you could get two Kit Kats or a big bag of popcorn. For a shilling you could eat for the entire movie on stuff that would 'rot your teeth and give you diabetes to boot', as my Granny used to say. She had a mild case of diabetes and related almost everything she could think of in the way of food to either getting or preventing the disease. Then we'd head upstairs after making sure that everyone had enough rolls of caps for their guns.

Opera House was a different kind of movie theater. In the old days it had really been an opera house where people sang on a big stage and where plays and concerts were held in front of fancy-dressed women and men. Then movies came along and Opera House got into them. My dad told me stories about Opera House. He told me about how he used to go there when he was a kid too. He said in those days the movies were silent and a girl named Marie Swan used to play unscripted, spontaneous music for stories involving Hoot Gibson and Buster Keaton and a lot of other dead guys. I didn't really understand how that could work so he tried to explain it to me.

"Remember when you're watching the *Durango Kid* serials and the Durango Kid is chasing the bad guys on his horse and..."

"It's usually the Durango Kid and his trusty sidekick Smiley Burnette who chase the bad guys together," I said.

"Yes, well, all right. When the Durango Kid and Smiley Burnette are chasing the bad guys on their horses the music speeds up in time with the horses galloping and the guns shooting and the Durango Kid hollering..."

"The Durango Kid never hollers. Smiley Burnette does sometimes, but the Durango Kid never hollers."

My dad took a deep breath and closed his eyes for a second. I figured he was picturing the olden days.

"Okay, so maybe it's Smiley Burnette and the bad guys hollering. And when the Durango Kid catches them the music slows down because the action has slowed down and you can hear them talking and—"

"Usually they're not talking because when the Durango Kid captures the bad guys and ties 'em up they don't really ever say anything. They just sit on the ground looking mad."

Dad shook his head and held his breath again. I heard him say "I'll just count to three," real quietly but I still heard him, although I wasn't sure why he wanted to count to three and not go higher.

"Anyway," he said after a while, "when I went to the movies at Opera House and there was a part where cowboys were chasing the bad guys Marie would start playing really fast and whenever things slowed down she'd slow down too. She just kept pace with the action, the same as they do in the movies you see today, except that then it wasn't part of the film. It was part of Opera House."

I still couldn't understand it, though.

"You couldn't hear anybody talk. How could you even understand what was going on if you couldn't hear anybody talk?"

"They had writing on the screen to tell you what the actors were saying. That way you could follow what was going on."

"But how about those kids in the audience who couldn't read?"

Dad nodded and his eyes went far away for just a moment and I hear him murmur under his breath "Not just the kids. Not just the kids." And he said it in a sad kind of way and for some reason I felt that he was remembering back to the old days when he used to sit in Opera House and read the words on the screen, and I wondered how many of his friends could do the same.

Then he looked at me and said "True, there were some there who never had the opportunity to go to school, never had the chance to learn how to read. Bermuda was different in those days, especially for some of us. But our piano player was good, and she could tell what the actors were saying even before the writing came up. So even if you couldn't read you could generally tell by the music what was going on."

My dad told me that Opera House had been built a really long time ago. It had been built by black men because in those days they didn't have any buildings they could actually call their own. All the others were owned by white people who didn't want black people inside them. The black men built Opera House so they could have a place where they could entertain and be entertained by black people, just like them.

"Were the black men slaves," I asked my dad.

He smiled, but it wasn't a good smile. It looked like the smile he put on when he got bowled out during one of his cricket games.

"No, they weren't slaves, son, they'd been free for a couple of decades." Then he shrugged his shoulders and smiled that same smile again. "But in fact they weren't really that far from slavery, not really free at all."

What my dad told me made Opera House even more special for me, even more unique. When we were kids it was the only movie theater in Bermuda where black people could sit upstairs in the balcony. Every other theater was segregated and if you were black you sat downstairs or nowhere.

But there were other things that made Opera House different. You could take your dog in with you, which was great for a kid if you didn't mind fleas. It wasn't unusual to look around about half way through the movie and see a whole balcony full of kids twitching and scratching, all eyes focused on the action on the screen.

When things got exciting in the movie the dogs joined in too, and when we started hollering and cheering and screaming and the dogs started barking the sound of the movie was completely drowned out. Then the screen would go dark and the lights would go up and the manager would walk down the aisle and come out on stage. And that's when every gun was removed from its holster and checked for its load of caps, because we knew what was coming next and so did the manager.

He'd hold up both hands and the noise would die down, just a bit, and he'd shout the words we were waiting to hear:

"If you kids don't quiet down and stop your noise we're going to end the movie right now."

And then all the yelling and the hollering and the barking would stop and silence would descend on Opera House. For ten seconds. Then every hand that held a gun would raise it high and the sound of hundreds of cap guns firing in the air would fill the theater. And the crescendo of noise would rise in a wave of sound as all of us chanted in voices as loud as we could:

"We want our money back! We want our money back!"

And the dogs would join in and the manager would wave his hands pleadingly and then leave the stage in exasperation and frustration. Then the lights would dim, the screen would brighten, the shouting would fade, the dogs would sit still and we'd watch the rest of the movie. It was an Opera House ritual and it happened every Saturday.

Opera House — it had dogs and fleas and films that broke in the most exciting parts. It had rickety wooden seats worn thin by the backs and bums of countless occupants. It had bare spots in the floor where carpet had once lain. It smelled of cigarettes, stale popcorn, dogs and unwashed kids. It had a balcony where we could sit and aisles where we could run and dance. It had a grumpy manager who'd let you in for sixpence if you didn't have a shilling. And it had Rickie Ratteray. That was Opera House, and we loved it.

Chapter 5
The Pact

Jay Jay's house was one of the most important houses on the Hill — it was the home of Jay Jay's comic book collection. That made it one of the most popular places for us kids to congregate. We'd get together around the comic book trunk in Jay Jay's bedroom and Jay Jay would wait until he was sure he had everyone's attention and then he'd reach down, snap off the clasp and pop open the top with a flourish. And as the lid went up and the stash of comics was revealed to our hungry eyes he'd say "Wallah!" just like he did every time. We asked him why he said "Wallah" whenever he opened the trunk with a flourish and what it meant. He said he heard a magician at the Agricultural Exhibition a couple of years ago say 'Wallah' when he pulled a rooster out of a straw hat and he thought it sounded really cool. He didn't know what it meant but that was okay because as long as it sounded cool that was good enough for him. We thought it sounded kind of stupid but no one was going to point that out to the keeper of the comics.

I was kind of curious about it so I asked my sister what it meant and she said she had absolutely no idea. Then she thought a bit and asked me where I'd heard the word. I told her about Jay Jay saying it and where he heard it and she shook her head and said "Jay Jay, I might have known." Then she laughed and said "It wasn't 'Wallah' the man at the Exhibition said, it was 'Voila'. It's a French word and it means something like 'Here it is'. Magicians use it all the time."

My sister knew a whole lot of French words because she'd been reading Beginners French books for a couple of years and was starting to read some that were even harder. She was super-smart and super-pretty too, but when it was your sister super-smart was a lot more important.

Anyway, after Jay Jay opened the trunk he'd reach in and take out a handful of comics and we'd sift through them, pick out one or two that we liked, go outside and find a spot on his porch steps and sit and read. When we finished the one we were reading we swapped with one of the other kids until all of us had read every comic in the bunch.

We were all sitting on the steps and reading and turning pages when Arnold looked up and said "Huh!" loud enough so that we all looked up too and then we just stared, because standing at the bottom of the steps staring back at us was a kid. But this was no ordinary kid. This kid had wavy red hair, bright blue eyes and light brown freckles all over his face. He was definitely not a Hill kid and he was definitely not a St. David's Island kid. This kid was white. Pure, pale, wishy-washy white.

After a while we got tired of him standing there staring at us and us sitting there staring at him and I said, "Who are you and where did you come from?" And he said, "I'm Zack and I came from Scotland."

We'd all heard of Scotland, just like we'd all heard of the moon, and someone coming from Scotland and standing there right in front of us was almost as strange and interesting as if he said he actually came from the moon. As far as we were concerned they could have been the same distance away. This was actually better because we all knew that anyone who came from the moon would definitely speak a different language, and at least a kid from Scotland would speak English. We soon found out that even if Scotland was on earth it didn't mean that Zack really could speak English, at least not the kind we were used to. He spoke sort of funny, almost in a sing song voice and the way he said words with 'r' in them was really weird.

He said he lived on the other side of the Hill down near Mrs. Cromwell and he'd only been in Bermuda about a week. He came from Scotland with his parents because his dad was a doctor and he got a job at the King Edward the Seventh Hospital in Paget. They spent almost the whole week travelling around the island, 'getting to know the place a wee bit be'uh'. He said things like 'wee' and 'och' and 'aye' a whole lot, but we figured that people must talk like that all the time in Scotland so we just let him go on.

After a week, though, he realized something that we kids knew all along — on Mrs. Cromwell's side of the hill down where she and Zack's family lived there was one thing that was missing, one important thing — kids. None of the people who lived down there had any kids anywhere near his age to play with, so he set off on his own to find some, and after a 'wee bit o' heearrd sirchin,' he'd found us.

Zack finished his story and stood very still and looked kind of hopefully at us. Then Jay Jay got up and said, "You know you're white, right?"

Zack grinned and said "I was this morning when I woke up."

"Just checking," Jay Jay laughed and waved him over to the steps. "You like comics?"

"Och aye."

"'That mean 'Yes'?"

Zack nodded.

"You got any favourites?"

"Aye...yes, yes indeed. I have. Y'see, in Scotland all the kids are crazy about the wild west, cowboys and Indians and that sort of thing, mainly because we never had cowboys and Indians in our country and they're really strange and wonderful to us. And I do have one particular favourite cowboy that you've probably never heard of way out here in

Bermuda, but we see him from time to time in the cinemas back home."

"Who's that?" I asked.

Zack smiled and, in a move as fast as lightning, he pulled two imaginary six shooters from two imaginary holsters and fired six imaginary shots into the air. We stared in awe and disbelief because we all recognized that quick draw style and knew that he could have copied it from only one person in the whole, wide world.

"The Durango Kid," Zack said, "the fastest gun in the West."

By the end of the afternoon Zack was the newest member of the Hill Gang.

In time Zack became one of my best friends for life. Now, it's true that when you're just a kid best friends for life sometimes last only about four or five months until another best friend for life comes along. But at that age four or five months is a pretty long time, and it was long enough for Zack and me to make The Pact. But before we made The Pact there was something else that had to be done, and it was something really important.

We were in the backyard at my house building forts out of limestone and sand for our armies of lead soldiers. Zack had an army that was kind of neat because they'd all come out of the same box so that they all matched and they all looked really sharp. Except for one thing — they all wore skirts, which was kind of a disadvantage when his soldiers were up against any other soldiers who didn't wear skirts · in other words, every other soldier in every other army that wasn't Zack's.

Zack had brought it on himself, though, because he'd pestered his mom to buy him a brand new set of soldiers so he wouldn't have an army like the rest of us, one made up of raggedy remnants of Union and Confederate army collections, marine platoons, Indian tribes, cowboys and any other soldiers we'd scavenged over time by trading, buying, borrowing and even stealing, some missing arms, some missing legs, some even missing heads.

So his mom did what any mom from Scotland would probably have done — she bought him a big, boxed set of Scottish soldiers. They were all very new and all very shiny and not one of them was missing a single body part. But they all had on skirts. And it didn't matter when Zack tried to explain that they weren't really skirts and that Scottish soldiers were some of the fiercest fighters in the world. As far as all of us were concerned he was stuck with a bunch of girly-guy soldiers.

But because we all needed an army to defeat, especially since our soldiers were generally badly wounded because of the missing parts, we let him participate in our battles and of course he always lost, no matter what. None of us could lose to soldiers in skirts. It was a matter of honour and pride.

The battles lost and won didn't stop Zack and me from being best friends for life. Only one thing could have, and so we had to take care of that by doing that really important thing that I mentioned before — we had to become brothers. And since he really wasn't my brother we had to do the next best thing — we had to become blood brothers. I knew all about how to do it and everything because I'd seen it in Jay Jay's comics, the Cowboys and Indians ones. All we had to do was cut our thumbs with a knife and join them together and share our blood.

So as I said, we were playing in my back yard when I brought up the subject. "Zack, you're my best friend, my really best friend, and we should be best friends for life."

"For life," Zack said, nodding his head and picking his nose, which is hard to do at the same time, if you think about it. I waited until he found what he was looking for, rolled it around in his fingers, flicked it up in the air and watched it bounce on the ground.

"You know what, Zack, I think we should be blood brothers, considering we're going to be best friends for life."

"Okay," he said, going for the other nostril, concentrating on the search this time, not nodding.

"First, we need a knife." This caused Zack to take his finger out and look at me a little more closely.

"A knife?"

"Uh huh. To make the cut."

I had his attention. He wiped his finger on his shorts.

"What cut?"

"Our thumbs. We have to cut our thumbs."

"With a knife?"

I could tell by the look on Zack's face that the whole idea of being a blood brother was rapidly losing its appeal. I wasn't worried, because I knew I had the convincer, the one thing that would get him to do it, and I used it.

"That's the way the Durango Kid always did it."

"He did?"

"Yep. With the Indians."

That was my secret weapon. Zack not only worshipped the Durango Kid, he actually wanted to *be* the Durango Kid when he grew up. I wasn't sure if Indians really did cut their thumbs or if they even knew what being a blood brother was. I thought I'd seen it in a serial one Saturday at Opera House but I wasn't sure. It could have been the Lone Ranger and Tonto, who was an Indian and only spoke two words in Indian and none in English, although Stan said 'Kemo Sabay' was actually Italian, and if anyone knew what they meant Stan would. But mentioning the Durango Kid worked, of course, and Zack wavered.

"I don't know," he said, wavering. I saw Zack was looking kind of doubtful so I nodded a lot and said, "Yep, the Durango Kid did it all the time." Zack stared at me really hard trying to see if there was the slightest chance that I was lying. I was prepared for that and already put on my honest face, which wasn't hard to do because I used it quite a bit in a lot of different circumstances. It never hurt to practice your honest face 'cause you never knew when you might have to use it.

"Okay'" Zack said, giving in. "Okay. If that's what the Durango Kid did."

I didn't want to give him time to think some more, so I ran into the house and looked in my mom's drawer that held all the knives. I didn't realize there were so many. I poked around in the drawer and took out the biggest one I could find. I looked at it closely. I ran my finger along the edge. I felt how sharp it was. I put it back. I took out the next biggest one and held it up to the light streaming in through the window. The light was gold from the sun and it flashed off the blade and danced in my eyes. I touched the edge. I put it back. I did that with all the knives until I reached the smallest one in the drawer. It was a paring knife my mom used to cut the ends off carrots. I looked at it and put it back.

By the time I got back outside Zack was wavering again but he looked at me, especially my hands, with a mixture of bravery and apprehension. Or maybe it was just apprehension.

"Where is it?"

"What?"

"The knife."

"I couldn't find one. Well, not the right one."

Zack's eyes lit up and he smiled.

"So I guess we're not going to be blood brothers." His relief was obvious.

"Of course we are. This is what we're going to use."

I held out my arm, a look of triumph on my face.

Zack grabbed my hand and pulled it closer to get a better look. He stared at me.

"A pin?"

'Uh huh."

"A pin?"

"Uh huh. It should do."

Zack nodded. "It should."

And so we went with the pin. We decided it would be best to prick our own thumbs, just to be on the safe side. Afterwards we smiled and told each other it didn't hurt at all, but it did, just a bit.

We put our thumbs together really carefully because a dot of blood the size of the head of a pin would have been easy to miss, especially when both our hands were trembling. We rubbed them together and smeared what little blood there was and declared ourselves blood brothers for life. And then we made The Pact. The Pact that sometime, anytime at all, Zack could ask me to do something really important, something that he really wanted done, something that no one else would do, and I would have to do it. And I could ask the same of him. We held our thumbs together again and swore that we would never, ever break The Pact. And later, much later, Zack fulfilled his part of The Pact. He killed my mom. But it was okay — I asked him to.

Chapter 6
Flying High

Two hundred and forty five restless, squirming, wriggling, impatient bums attached to two hundred and forty five restless, squirming, wriggling, impatient kids. And their parents.

We were in Pembroke Church waiting impatiently for the minister, not waiting for him to start his sermon but to finish it. And he knew how we felt, which was why it seemed to us like he was deliberately dragging it out. Of course this day was one of the most important days for him and for all of us agonizing in the pews as well. But it was important for far different reasons. For the minister it was one of the saddest days of the year — Good Friday. For us it was one of the happiest — Good Friday. The minister's face was somber and grim as he spoke about Jesus nailed to a wooden cross, about the pain and suffering he endured. If he looked more closely at us in the congregation he would have figured out pretty quickly that we were enduring some pain and suffering too.

Ours wasn't related to Jesus getting hung up on a cross. Ours had everything to do with the fact that this day, this special day, this Good Friday day, was

Kite Day. And Kite Day in Bermuda was like no other kite day anywhere else in the world. In the rest of the world you could fly a kite any time you wanted, any day you wanted, and I guess you could have done the same in Bermuda. In fact, sometimes you might see a kite flying, but you'd only see one or two and they'd be in the sky only a day or two before or after Good Friday.

On Good Friday, though, if the wind was up and it wasn't raining the sky would be full of kites, and the kites would be Bermuda kites. My mom said that in the early days the kite frames were made in the shape of a cross, much like they are today, and the reason was that when they flew they represented Jesus going up into heaven, or something like that. I never really paid much attention to that part. I just liked kites.

Bermuda kites were the prettiest kites in the world. They came in different shapes, from round to hexagonal to box shapes, and they ranged in size from as small as a matchbox to as tall as a house. And they were all made in Bermuda, not like those shiny plastic kites that the kids who lived on the American base at Kindley Field or up at the U S Naval Operating Base in Southampton used to bring in from the States.

Ours were made from specially cut sticks of wood. We got the sticks from Jay Jay's dad. He was a carpenter and his workshop was in a building beside their house. In the days leading up to Good Friday he was the hero of the Hill, because nobody could cut kite sticks like Jay Jay's dad. Kite sticks had to be just the right length, just the right width, and just the right thickness for the size of kite you were going to make, and Jay Jay's dad was an expert at sawing the sticks.

We hung around his shop watching him work, waiting for him to finish whatever he was doing in his regular job so he could start on our sticks. Every now and then he'd look up from his carpenter's bench and see all these eyes staring at him hungrily like a bunch of starving animals. This happened every day after school in the two weeks leading up to Good Friday. Sometimes he held out for a few days, letting the anticipation and anxiety build. Then it got to the point where he just couldn't stand the anxious, upturned faces and the pleading eyes anymore and he'd cut the kite sticks and we'd go home, happy and ready to make our kites.

After we put the frame together we made different designs with string and then covered them with brightly-coloured tissue paper that we glued to the string and the wood sticks. We put hummers on the kites so they'd sing in the air. We cut up old pillow cases or worn out bed sheets into strips for the kite tail, tied the tail onto the tail loop and then they were ready to fly. And our kites had one really big advantage over all the other non-Bermuda plastic kites that all the other non-Bermuda kids had — they flew.

And they flew high, really high, and they flew for a long time. If the wind was right, if it was steady and fairly strong, then a lot of people left their kites up all night and didn't bring them down until Saturday morning.

There was one rule, however, that all we kids had to obey. One rule that all we kids had to endure. One rule that all we kids hated. The rule that said before any of us could do any kite flying on Good Friday we had to go to church. It didn't matter if you didn't go to church on any other day of the year - Good Friday was one day that you went. And this rule was strictly enforced - for the kids. For the parents it wasn't so strict, although a lot of them went, probably because they were brainwashed when they were kids like us and couldn't get out of the habit. My mom went sometimes, my dad never did. I wanted to be just like him when I grew up.

But I wasn't grown up yet, and like all the other kids in church I sat, squirmed and wriggled impatiently until the minister finally got down from the pulpit. We all sang 'The Old Rugged Cross', said a few 'Amens', and then it was over.

The doors opened, sunlight streamed through and we knew that at last we were free. I'm not sure about the grownups but I knew that every one of us kids wanted to run out of there 'like bats out of hell', as my dad used to say. We could almost feel the kite strings in our hands, see them flying high in the bright, blue Bermuda sky, hear the hummers buzzing in the wind.

But we knew from experience that dashing for the doors was not going to happen, because our parents knew the score and they were ready. As soon as the service was over a hand clamped down on the shoulder of every kid in the building, a restraining hand, a hand that made sure that all of us left the church in as dignified a manner as possible. And we did, until we cleared the doors, and then we were gone.

Stan and me ran up the Hill as fast as our legs could move, thoughts of kites dancing in our heads. By the time our moms got home our kites were ready, and we waited just long enough for them to slice the hot cross buns, butter them, make fish sandwiches and put them in a paper bag with a bottle of mineral. My mom tried to get us to wait awhile because she said she felt something in the air, but we knew it was just a stalling tactic and she wasn't fooling us one little bit.

Then we were out the door and dashing down the Hill to meet the rest of the Gang. We got together on the field on the other side of Northlands primary school and we were the first to get there. We knew that if we were early we'd get a good spot to pitch our kites and get them in the air without anyone else interfering with our space. We placed our kites gently on the grass and put on the tails and tied on the strings to fly them with.

And then something happened. Something worse than a long Good Friday sermon in church. Something worse than a Gene Autry movie at Opera House. Something worse than a Louie Butterfield haircut on a Durango Kid Saturday.

The wind died. Died completely. Not a breath of a breeze was left in the air and as everybody knew — without wind there was no hope of flying a kite. We planned for this day, hoped for this day, waited for this day, anticipated this day, and now it was ruined.

"Maybe it was church," Jay Jay said. We looked at him but didn't say anything because we knew that there was more to come. With Jay Jay there was always more to come.

"You know, the way we acted. Maybe it was God. Maybe we didn't show enough respect to his kid, um, you know, to Jesus."

Stan stared at him for a little bit, until Jay Jay looked down at his kite lying dead on the ground.

Stan shook his head. "Not enough respect? Not enough respect? Look, we went to church when we didn't want to. We sang a whole bunch of hymns when we didn't want to. We listened to the longest, most boring Good Friday sermon in the entire world when we didn't want to. We walked out of church as slowly and as quietly as we could when we didn't want to. We spent the entire morning doing all those things that we didn't want to do because Jesus got crucified on a hill a million years ago. And on top of that we were going to do the only thing that we all really wanted to do, which was to fly our kites basically in his honour. Now how much more respect do you think Jesus deserved?"

As usual, Stan was right and even Jay Jay couldn't argue with his logic. We sat and ate our fish sandwiches and waited for the wind to come, but it didn't. An hour later, after we'd eaten all the sandwiches and drunk all the pop we knew it was hopeless.

Jay Jay got up and spat on the ground one more time for good luck.

"I just wish we had some wind, just a little bit of wind," he said, and as if by magic as soon as he said it a gentle breeze blew in from the ocean, building as it got to the field into a real kite wind. Everyone on the field started whooping and shouting, pitching their kites in the air and running with the lines. All over the field kites climbed into the sky and there was joy on everyone's face.

Stan looked at Jay Jay and grinned. "If it was God I guess he's stopped being mad."

And we cheered and laughed and watched our kites dancing in the air.

As time passed the wind wasn't content to just be a kite wind. It grew stronger and stronger until people began to get concerned and started to pull their kites down before the wind broke the lines and took the kites away. I wasn't worried about the wind, and my kite was flying higher and higher.

"You should bring it in," Stan said, but I was too excited watching it weave back and forth. It was so much higher than anyone else's, mainly because everyone else was bringing their kites down, pulling them in against the ever-increasing wind. But not me, mine was doing just fine.

"I've got super-strong line," I told Stan. "Nothing can break it." I watched my kite soaring higher and higher and felt it pulling really hard on the line.

"Do you think they fly kites in heaven?" I asked him.

"Sure they do, especially on Good Friday. And they never have to worry about the wind or the rain because there's always just the right amount of wind and there's never any rain."

"Huh. It must be great up there on Good Friday, everyone flying their kites. Probably a lot like down here, only nicer."

By now all the other kites were down and people were hurrying to get them to shelter before the wind could blow holes in the tissue paper.

"You really should take in your kite before it breaks away," Stan said again. "The wind is getting too strong."

"Don't worry; I just want another couple of minutes, then I'll bring it down. It just looks so pretty up there all by itself, with no other kites around."

"You're just showing off," he said, which was absolutely true, and just as I was about to say I wasn't I felt the line go slack in my hand. I glanced down at it to see what happened then up to see all my line floating down across the field. I looked up at my kite and it was spiralling higher and higher in the sky, no longer attached to the line. I stared in disbelief, looked around and saw all the other kids staring too, their mouths and eyes wide open.

Soon my kite was a tiny speck over the ocean, the colours no longer visible, just a black dot growing smaller and smaller every second. I blinked and looked again and couldn't find it.

"It's gone," Jay Jay said. "It's gone."

And he was right. My kite had disappeared.

And then it came, starting in my chest and spreading all through my body, a feeling as warm and comforting as any I'd ever had, as warm and comforting as when my mom used to hold me in her arms on those damp and cold March evenings at home on the Hill. And then I knew why my kite broke away, and what it was my mom felt in the air.

And I started to smile and I couldn't stop. Stan looked at me strangely and asked me if I was okay. I said "Yes."

"You just lost your kite, the prettiest kite of them all. Why are you smiling?"

I shook my head. "No, Stan, I didn't lose it. You said they fly kites in heaven and I know that's where mine is now, and I know who's flying it. That's why I'm smiling."

"Who's flying it?"

"David," I said. "David's flying it."

Chapter 7
Mrs. Cromwell's Loquats

Mrs. Cromwell lived almost at the bottom of the Hill, on the other side from where Jay Jay and Jackie lived. We didn't know Mrs. Cromwell very well, maybe because she was white and old and lived alone and looked a lot like the witches we'd seen in one of Jay Jay's comic books. A teacher gave him the book when she heard he collected comics and told him it was educational. It was about a guy in England or Ireland or somewhere like that who lived a long time ago and his wife was really bad and he had blood on his hands or maybe she did and they couldn't sleep very well and killed people.

There was a neat part about a marching forest too, but it was the witches that were the coolest. They were mean and ugly with black pointed hats; long, knobby noses; fiery, evil eyes and wrinkled, shrivelled-up faces. And even if Mrs. Cromwell didn't have a pointed hat we knew that in every other way she looked exactly like the witches in Jay Jay's comic book. Even though none of us really ever got a good look at her because she stayed in the house a lot and we hardly ever saw her come out and when she did we hid in the bushes because we were afraid of her.

Even though we were afraid of her we couldn't stay away from her house, especially at one particular time of the year, because there was something in her backyard that attracted us like flies to poop. A loquat tree. But hers was not just any loquat tree. We investigated a lot of loquat trees in our travels around Pembroke Parish, which was basically the extent of the known world for us kids, and on Mrs. Cromwell's tree were the biggest, sweetest, juiciest loquats that any of us ever tasted. And every spring we stole them.

Loquat trees exploded with all kinds of flowers in December. By January little green loquats replaced the flowers. By February the loquats weren't so little anymore and by the middle of March they were full grown and turning yellow-orange and getting ready for eating. And if you never tasted a loquat ... well, I can't describe the taste very well except loquats tasted better than any type of fruit we ever ate. One of the things that made them so special was that they only lasted for a couple of weeks before they turned black and fell off the trees so we needed to get them when we could, and the best place to get them was from the tree in Mrs. Cromwell's back yard.

Except for one thing — Mrs. Cromwell herself, the witch-guardian of the loquat tree. She'd been through loquat season before. She knew us kids, she knew how we felt about her loquats and we knew that she knew we were just a gang of sneaky, little loquat thieves. So she watched over that tree like a mamma lion watched over her cubs, watched it through her kitchen window every chance she got, and if she had Superman eyes she could have looked into the bushes on the Hill and seen seven pairs of eyes watching her watching the tree.

We were terrified of being caught but we wanted those loquats more than we wanted to see the new *Durango Kid* movie at Opera House, more than we wanted to read one of Jay Jay's new *Bat Man* comics, and we were ready to risk anything to get them. Anything, except being caught by the witch. And so we waited for our chance and through experience we knew it would come. Mrs. Cromwell would have to leave the kitchen some time. There was laundry to do, the house to clean, and even witches had to pee.

Trouble was we never knew exactly when any of those things would happen, so we waited for the slightest opportunity and when it came we struck. But we didn't strike without a plan. We definitely had a plan, developed and perfected over at least two loquat seasons and tested many times during the weeks of loquat ripeness. The plan was actually quite simple and it depended entirely on two things.

One was the way the loquats grew on the tree, and the other was the collective will of seven little kids.

See, other than Mrs. Cromwell there was another problem. Everybody who knows loquats knows that the best ones grow way out on the end of the branches, but the lowest branches on Mrs. Cromwell's tree were about three feet higher off the ground than Stan could reach, and he was the tallest. We solved that with our plan.

As soon as Mrs. Cromwell left the kitchen we snapped into action. One of us was assigned as a lookout. Five of us climbed up on to the branch with the most fruit at the end and took our places in line, holding on to the branch above us so we wouldn't fall off. We couldn't go all the way out where the loquats were because the end of the branch wasn't big enough to support even the smallest member of our Gang — which was me. Five little black kids all in a row. We looked like crows on a telephone wire.

Then at a signal from Stan we put our plan into action. He said "Go" and we all jumped up and down on the branch. We did this until we got the timing right, until the branch was moving up and down in a nice, slow rhythm. Then Stan went out to the end of the branch and reached up his arms and we bounced the loquats right into his hands.

He had to be pretty quick because the loquats were only at his level for a second before the branch snapped back up. But he was Stan and he was quick and as the branch came down he just picked off one bunch of loquats and waited until it came back down again. Finally a signal from our lookout told us when Mrs. Cromwell was back in the kitchen and moving toward the window. We were off that branch and into the bushes in a flash and spent the next half hour or so eating loquats and watching Mrs. Cromwell watching the tree. And smiling.

It was all so cool, but like a lot of cool things that happen to kids it didn't last, and it was all because of Stan. He was always thinking of ways to improve things, and getting loquats off Mrs. Cromwell's tree was no exception. What he figured was if we leaped up high enough and came down hard enough he could grab the branch rather than the loquats. Then we could jump off while he held it down and all have a go at picking. That way we'd get a lot more loquats in a lot shorter time and we wouldn't have to worry half as much about Mrs. Cromwell.

Well, we all agreed that was a really great idea and we decided to pick a really big branch with really big bunches of loquats hanging off the end. We climbed up on the branch, Stan stood ready on the ground and we began to jump. The branch was very thick and it took a lot of jumps before we even got it moving. But move it did, just a little at first but we were determined to make Stan's idea work. So we jumped higher and higher and we landed harder and harder and the branch dipped lower and lower until — success. The branch sank down to its lowest point and Stan reached up to grab it and when he did he wrapped his arms around it as tight as he could. We gave a yell of triumph and leaped onto the ground and that's when tragedy struck.

Without our weight to keep it down the end of the branch snapped back up like a whip. We could hear it whoosh through the air and watched in amazement at how high it actually went. And we watched in wonder as Stan flipped off the end like a bug and soared into the air. Afterwards Jay Jay said he thought Stan looked just like Superman, except for his shorts and T-shirt and dirty sneakers and the fact he wasn't white.

He flew through the branches and we could hear them crackling and snapping as he went up. And we could hear them crackling and snapping as he came down. He hit the ground with a thud and a howl and we saw that his right leg was bent at an angle that no leg, right or left, was supposed to bend.

It was Mrs. Cromwell who came and lifted Stan up and carried him into her kitchen. It was Mrs. Cromwell who called the ambulance and our parents. It was Mrs. Cromwell who gave us bread and molasses and chocolate milk while we sat and watched and waited. It was Mrs. Cromwell who wrapped Stan in a blanket and gave him aspirins and talked quietly to him until the ambulance came and took him away.

And sitting in her kitchen on that strange and sunny afternoon we found out some things that completely changed how we felt about Mrs. Cromwell and taught us an important lesson too — though I'm not real sure about Jay Jay, who kept looking around for comic books which he said afterwards would probably have been really old and really cool.

We found out that Mrs. Cromwell did watch the tree from her kitchen window each loquat season, and she did know we kids would be coming. What we didn't realize was that she looked forward to seeing us, that she relished our enjoyment because it gave her joy, that she laughed at what she called our 'antics.' We weren't sure what that meant but Jay Jay said afterwards he thought she meant a cross between ants and ticks and the way they moved, jumping and crawling and stuff.

Stan smacked him up side his head and said it was a grown-up word for the way we fooled around, and Stan was almost always right. Except for his idea to get the loquats. But Mrs. Cromwell said there was one thing that disappointed her. Every time she went near the window or started to go outside we all disappeared like magic so she never got a chance to speak to us.

And there was something else we found out — Mrs. Cromwell somehow changed. Her nose was no longer long and pointed and knobby, but small and pink and straight. Her fiery, evil eyes were now soft and blue and warm, and strangest of all, her shriveled, wrinkled, witch's face became round and smooth and kind.

We went down to Mrs. Cromwell's house a lot after that. We ran errands for her and helped her with chores and kept her yard tidy and clean. We ate her molasses bread and drank her chocolate milk and we never stole another loquat from Mrs. Cromwell's tree.

We didn't have to.

Chapter 8
Not too High and Not too Close

Saturday, when you got to sleep in as late as you liked but got up earlier than any other day of the week because you didn't have to. Saturday, when there was not even a hint of school in the air. Saturday, when your mom handed out your two shilling six pence allowance. Saturday, when Opera House showed the latest installment in the *Durango Kid* serial. Saturday, when you got one of your two favourite meals of all time — hot dogs or hamburgers. Saturday, when both the *Royal Gazette* and the *Mid Ocean News* had full pages of comics. Saturday, the most amazing and wonderful day of the week. Except for the one day when Saturday became something to dread, simply because of two things — haircuts and Louie Butterfield. Haircuts only happened once every two months but they happened on a Saturday. Louie Butterfield was one of the meanest, nastiest, weirdest people on the island.

Louie Butterfield was the barber.

The problem was that Louie gave really good haircuts. Some said they were the best on the island. Therefore, to get one of the best haircuts on the island you had to put up with Louie, his meanness, his nastiness, and his really strange habits. Since most of the parents on the Hill wanted their kids to get a good haircut they sent us to Louie. Although our parents always taught us to be polite and not to call adults by their first names none of us ever called him Mr. Butterfield, and none of our parents ever corrected us. As a person Louie wasn't held in much esteem. As a barber, though, it was different.

Louie lived in a house down on the North Shore but it wasn't Louie's house we went to for our haircuts. Because, as Louie put it, he didn't want 'no frizzy bits of wiry-assed kid's hair scattered like chicken shit all over his living room floor,' he did his haircutting in a shed in his back yard.

If you were going for a haircut at Louie's you had to make sure you didn't plan anything for the entire Saturday, no matter what time you got there. That meant no Opera House, no movie, no popcorn, no candy bar, no orange pineapple mineral, and worst of all, no *Durango Kid* serial. That was one of the reasons haircut Saturday was so terrible.

Louie lined the back and sides of his shed with concrete building blocks that he stood on end, and you had to sit on one of them and wait your turn to get your haircut. It seemed no matter how early you got there the shed was always full of kids, fidgeting and talking and looking at the lucky guy sitting in the barber chair being done by Louie. We called it a barber chair only because it was where you sat to get your haircut.

Louie was way too cheap to get a real barber chair so he used a forty-five gallon drum turned upside down with a tablecloth on top of it and a pillow on top of the tablecloth. The pillow was old and thin with half the insides missing so after about fifteen minutes your bum would start to get sore and the bottom of your legs would get marks from the rim of the barrel. And no haircut at Louie's lasted less than thirty minutes, no matter how much hair you had. My dad said Louie once took an hour and a half giving Mr. Hunt a haircut and Mr. Hunt was bald from birth. My dad was lying like he sometimes did, but you get the point.

Keeping the haircutting tools clean was not one of Louie's strong points or even one of his concerns. He didn't have a glass full of blue liquid that you put the combs and scissors in to sanitize them, like Jay Jay said they did in some real barbershops in Hamilton. He just shook any excess hair out of them and laid them on the workbench until he needed them for the next haircut.

His combs ran through the hair of every kid in the shed without ever being wiped off and you had to hope you got combed first before the kid with lice had his turn because there was always at least one kid with lice. And as for washing your hair either before or after your haircut, that never happened. You'd leave Louie's shed itching and scratching and hoping it was from the millions of little hairs down your neck and back and not because of some little white bugs transferred to you on one of Louie's combs.

Anyway, when your turn finally came he sat you on the barrel and started in one side at a time. But if there was a cricket game on the radio you were in for a long sit. See, Louie once played cricket, and my dad said he was one of the worst players ever. My dad played cricket and he was a really good wicket-keeper and batsman and according to him Louie couldn't hit a cricket ball with a goddamned tennis racket, he couldn't bowl a batsman out if the goddamn batter was blind and the goddamn wicket was two feet away, and he couldn't field a cricket ball if it was as big as a goddamn cantaloupe and laying dead on the goddamn ground. 'Goddamn' was probably my dad's favourite swearword, right next to 'Blad-of-a-bull'.

When I asked him what team Louie played for and why they chose him in the first place he said it was simple — Louie owned the team. He named them the Butterballs. My dad said he named them that because Louie thought people would connect the name not only to him but to cricket balls as well. Louie thought it was clever. My dad thought it connected to balls, all right, but not to the kind

Louie was thinking of. My mom said she thought the name was unfortunate.

Louie sponsored the team, bought all the equipment, paid the grounds fees for the fields and most important, bought the food and the booze for the team parties, all of which were held at his house. According to my dad, with Louie in the line-up the Butterballs lost every cricket match they ever played. Their record was not entirely hopeless, however. They did win two games during their brief existence, one when Louie was out with adult measles and one when he got drunk and fell down the stairs at the Somerset Cricket Club during Cup Match one year and was in a cast for a month.

Louie loved the game so much he played two games wearing the cast. The Butterballs lost them both. After that season every cricket league in Bermuda refused to let Louie enter a team, which was just as well since he couldn't get anybody to play for him anyway. The ones who never played for him before didn't want to ruin their reputations and the ones that had played and whose reputations were already ruined couldn't take the sneers and the jeers and the jokes anymore.

So if a cricket game came on the radio Louie would stop in mid-cut, drop his clippers, grab an imaginary bat and assume his stance in front of an imaginary wicket. Then he'd play beautiful strokes against the bowler on the radio, hitting sizzling fours and slamming towering sixes to all parts of the imaginary field inside his head. And if the batter on the radio got out Louie would just become the new batter. And if you were the unfortunate person sitting on the barrel or one of the kids sitting on the concrete blocks waiting your turn, you got to watch Louie stroke, run, swing and swear until the entire side was out. And that meant ten imaginary players you had to watch.

The most terrifying thing for us kids was when Louie decided to take his turn at bowling for the other team. He didn't use an imaginary ball for that, he used the electric clippers. He'd whip his arm around within inches of your head and you knew that if he decided to bowl an inswinger instead of a googly you might end up with a two-inch bald strip right down the middle of your head.

Finally, with the sweat dripping off his face making dirty splotches on the dusty floor Louie would lean his imaginary bat against the wall, wipe his face with an old washcloth and head for the house. You sat in the barber chair and waited. The kids sat on the concrete blocks and waited.

Louie would come back sucking on a glass of ice water, look around the room and then look at you in the chair like he'd never seen you before. Which was kind of scary because you'd be looking back at him with half the hair on your head cut off, and he was the one who did it. Then he'd pick up the clippers and your hopes would rise because it was still only 11:30 and the *Durango Kid* serial began at Opera House at 1 p.m. and maybe, just maybe, you'd get there. He'd start on the other half of your head and if you were lucky he'd get through the rest of your haircut without any interruptions and you still might make the serial.

All of us knew that the next great hurdle was lunch. Not ours — Louie's. And just like with cricket, when lunch came Louie went away. Not in his imagination — he actually went away. And you couldn't count on a set time when that would happen because Louie's wife cooked when she felt like it, so sometimes lunch could be at lunchtime, other times it might be at eleven in the morning or two in the afternoon, and Jay Jay said he was there one time when lunch was after four. Jay Jay said afterwards it might have been early supper, he couldn't tell.

If you couldn't count on when Louie's lunch would be ready there was one thing you could count on — no matter when lunch was served Louie would take the time to eat it. We were always prepared for this and so were our moms, and none of us ever went to Louie's without a paper bag stocked with peanut butter sandwiches and a bottle of mineral. So Louie would eat and we would eat and when we were all finished Louie would come back and the rest of your hair would get cut. Maybe.

And then there was the time something happened that almost resulted in Louie's death. Okay, maybe not his death, but I think it introduced Louie to a whole new understanding of what a near-death experience actually was, and I was an important part of the whole event. It happened because of three things that came together at the same time — a County Cup cricket match, lunch, and a haircut. My haircut.

Louie's wife made his lunch at the same time that his favourite player on the Bailey's Bay team took up the bowling duties for a spell, so Louie was conflicted. He was conflicted because his wife would never let him listen to a cricket match while he was in the house. She'd been a witness to some of the destruction caused by his imaginary participation in cricket matches and ordered him out of the house if he wanted to do three things: one - continue to live in their house; two - continue to live with her; three - continue to live. So Louie took his game outside.

She also laid down rules about breakfast, lunch and supper. When Louie was home all those meals had to be eaten inside the house. There was no taking anything out to eat in the shed or on the porch or on the lawn. Meals must be eaten in the house and there was no compromise. And meals could not be skipped. What she cooked must be eaten when she cooked it, and gulping the food to get away quicker was not allowed.

So this day Louie was conflicted. I was on the barrel, six other kids were waiting to get their hair cut, lunch was being served and his favourite bowler was taking his stride behind the wicket. Then he did the unthinkable. He made a mistake. Which was okay, because everyone makes mistakes. But he made a mistake with me, and that was the bad part — the really bad part.

What happened was he got mad because his favourite player just got bowled out for a duck. This got him so mad he started to wave his arms in the air and swear and try to bat and bowl at the same time. He looked like one of those Holy Roller people in the hall up by St. Monica's Road. He looked possessed, even more possessed than usual. He took a swipe in the air with the electric clippers and misjudged the distance to my head. What I ended up with was a shaved, two inch wide strip down the right side of my head, with a bit of a curve at the end. My head looked like a miniature version of Horseshoe Bay Beach — if Horseshoe Bay Beach had been surrounded on both sides by hair.

Louie knew that something was wrong, that something interfered with his otherwise perfect bowling delivery. He turned around and looked behind him but didn't notice anything because he was looking down at the floor. He shrugged, frowned, muttered under his breath and began his bowling motion again, in perfect time with the bowler on the radio. Just before he swept his arm up he noticed that he was a little too close to me and moved over a bit. Then he stopped suddenly in mid-bowl, lowered his arm and looked at my head. The look turned into a stare, the stare into a frown, the frown into a grimace.

A mistake, he made a mistake, a really big mistake and he knew it. Now his problem was how to correct it. What do you do with a kid sitting on your barber barrel with a two inch wide strip running down the side of his head going all the way down to his bare scalp?

All thoughts of the cricket game on the radio left Louie's head and you could almost smell him thinking, or maybe it was just sweat because it was running down his cheeks and his shirt was getting wet and dirty stains were beginning to show on it under his arms and on his chest. I kind of felt sorry for him because I knew why he was sweating.

Louie had his instructions and they were very simple and very clear — not too high and not too close. What it meant was he was not supposed to cut my hair too high above my ears and he was not supposed to cut it too close to my scalp. Like I said, the instructions were simple and clear but the part that was bothering Louie was the person who'd given him the instructions, the absolute worst person in the world who's simple and clear instructions you should never, ever not follow — my dad. That was why Louie was sweating. That was why Louie was afraid.

Louie was shaking a little when he looked me over. I was fine as far as the 'not too high' part went and three quarters of the haircut wasn't really too close, but then there was the one quarter part, the bald-right-down-to-the-scalp part, and eventually Louie came up with the only solution he could think of. He cut off the rest of my hair. All of it.

And then he waited.

I never went back to Louie for a haircut again, which was okay because it was a couple of months before they removed his cast. After that Louie only cut grownups' hair. My dad said he gave up his make-believe cricket games too because his arm healed kind of funny and now he couldn't bowl a good ball anyway.

He told me this in a really serious voice, but he had a smile on his face.

Chapter 9
Jillie

My sister's best friend was Melanie Shillington. We called her Mel and she was four years older than me and she had a sister named Julie Anne who was about as old as I was and we called her Jillie. Her parents never called them anything but Melanie and Julie Anne. They were very strict that way, and in other ways, too. Mrs. Shillington was small and skinny and had light skin and came from an island in the West Indies that none of us had ever heard of. My dad said it was French and told us its name and it sounded like a drink that my mom said my Uncle Wilfred liked way·y·y too much — Martini·something. Her hair was short and frizzy and her face looked like it had never been young.

Mr. Shillington was from Trinidad and he was the opposite of Mrs. Shillington, except for maybe his face. He was tall and big and black and he didn't have frizzy hair because he didn't have any at all and his face was unfriendly even when he smiled, which Jay Jay said afterwards only happened twice as far as he could remember. Jay Jay never stayed around Mr. Shillington long enough to see if he smiled more often.

Jillie was as pale as her mother and her hair was black and curly and she was pretty and kind of delicate. All us boys liked her a lot and if we'd been older we'd have probably liked her even more, in a different kind of way. But we never got the chance.

Jay Jay said afterwards he thought she might have been a Mohawk, which was another name for a person from St. David's Island, because St. David's Islanders were mixtures of every colour you could think of. They were called Mohawks because of their American Indian ancestors who were brought in as slaves long ago to help the black slaves do things that slaves do. My dad said one of the things they did really well was interbreed with black and white folks alike, resulting in some different-looking kids. Which is why even today some St. David's Islanders are pretty interesting to look at.

I had some cousins from there who were black with blue eyes and straight hair, and some who were as white as any white person could get but with crinkly red hair that no real white person ever had. Looking at what some white people did to their hair to make it curly they probably wished it had been crinkly right from the start, just maybe not red.

One of the things that made Jillie special was it seemed she existed apart from our kid's world, like she didn't really belong in it, although sometimes it seemed like she wanted to. She was distant and different, more silent and quiet than any of the other girls on the Hill. She didn't try to play with us — not with the boys, not with the girls. She'd just stand on her lawn and look at us while Mr. Shillington watched through his screen door, and his eyes were a wall between Jillie and us and when any of us stopped to say 'Hi' to her we'd see his face and just keep going.

We played marbles on a flat piece of road that ran along the side of their property. Although Jillie didn't play with us sometimes she came out and stood up on the bank on her lawn and watched. She'd smile just a little bit and we'd wave and she'd wave back but her wave was always small, like her smile. She never came too close to us, which was strange because we felt that maybe she really wanted to but just couldn't. We knew from the smile and the wave that she was friendly and we were pretty sure that she liked us, especially Jackie. And Jackie liked her too, a lot.

Some parents seem to have a special sense about kids who like their children, especially their daughters. Whenever Jackie was with us and Jillie was outside Jackie would wave and Jillie would smile and Jackie would start to speak to her. As soon as he saw that, Mr. Shillington would shove open the screen door he'd been looking through all the time and tell her to come inside. She'd go in right away and we'd watch her go and we'd look at the empty space she left behind and we'd miss her and worry a bit. We didn't really know why we worried and we couldn't explain why, not then, and not for a long while after. By the time we figured out the 'why' it was much too late, for us and for Jillie.

We were just boys. Girls were for tolerating, for not being like one of the boys, for talking to as long as you didn't have to do it for too long and the topic didn't involve dolls or playing doctor, which most of us wouldn't really appreciate until a couple of years later — playing doctor, I mean.

To us girls were just, well, girls. There was nothing really special about them, they certainly weren't what we wanted to be and they certainly didn't have anything that we boys wanted to have. We were just boys and we didn't know anything about the boy-girl connection that would become for most of us the most important connection ever. We were just boys.

Then one day something strange happened while we were playing marbles on the dirt road. I remember it because it was my turn to shoot and I was in a really great position to knock at least four marbles out of the ring. If you know anything about marbles then you know that any marble I knocked out of the ring with my bongy —which was a really big marble —belonged to me.

Everyone was looking at me because they knew I was a really good shooter so they were all worried about which marbles I was going for and hoping it wasn't theirs. I knew exactly which ones were going to be mine but I kept looking around and going 'Hmmm' and taking my time, just to get on their nerves. I learned how to do that from my mom who was really good at getting on people's nerves, but only when she wanted to.

And just when the silence had built up so great that the only thing you could hear was Jay Jay breathing through his mouth because he had a cold and his nose was full of snot and slime, just when I knew that I was the absolute center of attention, just when I was all set to send every marble in that ring flying, at that crucial point Jackie let out a gasp. It wasn't a gasp that had anything to do with my being a split second from releasing chaos and destruction with my mighty bongy. I knew that because two seconds beforehand Jackie was leaning over me to watch me shoot and the gasp didn't come from someone who was still leaning over me. It came from someone who was now standing straight up with his head turned away from me about as far as it could turn.

I looked up and saw that everyone's head was turned in the same direction as Jackie's, so I turned mine too and all of us were staring at Jillie. Jillie, who was right there on the road. Jillie, who wasn't standing up on the bank a safe distance away from us. Jillie, who was wearing a white dress and white shoes with her hair down onto her shoulders and a look on her face we never saw before. She looked happy.

I didn't believe in angels since my dad and I had a discussion involving God and Jesus and the church and them. He wasn't too sure whether he believed in God or Jesus but, as he put it, he sure as goddamn hell didn't believe in the church. I asked him why and he told me how the church thing started, about the time that he and Mr. Parsons decided to go to a Sunday service at the Parish Church, which was down below the Hill about a half mile from our house. Just to check something out was how my dad put it.

They got to the church just before the service began, walked right up to the front pew and sat down where you actually had to strain your neck to look up at the minister in the pulpit. According to my dad that buzz you always hear in church before the minister arrives suddenly stopped and things got really quiet, quieter than when you had a minutes silence at the Cenotaph in November in honour of the people who died in all the wars.

Then one of the deacons or someone who'd been blessed by the minister or someone else in close contact with God came up and told my dad and Mr. Parsons that they'd have to move. My dad said it was no problem since he and Mr. Parsons obviously made a mistake because the front pew was probably reserved for members of the choir or you deacon guys. What we'll do, he said, is we'll move one row back to the second pew. But the deacon guy said no, the second pew wasn't available either. As it turned out the only pews available to my dad and Mr. Parsons were in the back half of the church, even though most of those in the front half were empty.

See, the problem was that Mr. Parsons was black and my dad was half black. My dad was half black because his dad was white and my grandma was from St. David's Island and she was mostly native American Indian but my dad said she had some black in her too, like most St. David's Islanders. So the deacon guy quietly explained to my dad that they had to sit in the back of the Church because the front half was reserved for white Christians only.

My dad just smiled up at the deacon guy and told him in a voice loud enough so everyone in the church could hear, that all the white Christians, the minister and the deacon guy too, could kiss the darkest part of his half-black ass. Then he and Mr. Parsons walked down the aisle past all the white, staring faces in the front and the black ones in the back and strode out of the building. He never went to church again. Any church.

My dad told me these things so that I could think about them and decide if I still wanted to go to church myself. My mom got kind of upset because she thought I was too young to be making those kinds of decisions on my own, but my dad said that I was old enough and smart enough to make up my own mind. I went to the bathroom and I looked in the mirror. I had light brown skin and curly brown hair and dark brown eyes. There was no doubt about it — I was black. I was old enough, my dad had said, to make my own decision. I never went to church again either. I was seven.

Anyway, about angels. My dad and I talked about them too. In church, when I used to go, they were all over the place. In the windows, in paintings, in sculptures, everywhere. At Christmas it was even worse — they came out of the churches and into the stores in every form and shape you could think of and they all had two things in common — every one of them had wings and every one of them was white. My dad said that it had to be obvious, even to a seven year old, that if angels did exist and considering the number of people in Bermuda and the rest of the world who weren't white, that the majority of angels weren't white either, and if they weren't white they had to be coloured, whether black, brown, yellow or green. I was curious about the green ones but he didn't want to talk about it.

He did talk about the wings, though, and explained to me that nowhere in the Bible did it mention that angels had wings, that it was only a couple of hundred years ago that people began to paint angels with wings and the idea caught on. But the original angels in the Bible had no wings at all, so according to my dad it stood to reason that if they didn't have wings they couldn't fly, and if they couldn't fly they had to get to earth some other way because if you just fell from heaven, then — splat! Dead angel. So you had to figure that they either just stayed around in heaven doing angel work or they just didn't exist. I didn't know what kind of angel work they could do in heaven, seeing everything up there was supposed to be perfect right from the start, so I guess that was a big factor in leading me to just not believe in angels at all.

Until that afternoon when Jillie appeared.

She stood there all in white and the sun was behind her and it caught the edges of her dress and lit it up so it shimmered and glowed like golden wings and she was everything I figured an angel should be. Or could be, if they really tried.

For what seemed like the longest while nobody moved, not us, not Jillie. And then Jackie took a step toward her, and then another, walking almost in slow motion, and Jillie just stood there smiling as he came to her. And when he reached her he did something that none of us had ever seen him do before, that none of us could ever imagine him doing, that none of us had ever even thought of doing, at least not with anyone who wasn't our mother or grandmother or auntie.

He kissed her. He kissed her on her cheek. And then Jillie did something too, something we thought she would never, ever do. She kissed him back, but not on the cheek. She put one hand on each side of his face and kissed him right on the lips. A long kiss, a kiss that seemed to last and last, a kiss like my mom gave my dad after he got back from three weeks away working in England in Scotland Yard.

And then her hands left his face and quickly moved down and we heard Jackie gasp and saw him jump back so suddenly we all jumped back too, although we were about twenty yards away. And then Jillie wasn't smiling anymore and a look of hurt and disappointment came on her face and she turned and ran as fast as anyone we ever saw run and then we heard her kitchen door slam shut and we had lost her.

Jackie walked back to us just as slowly as he went to her but the look on his face wasn't the same. Surprise and disbelief was what was there, the same look that was on our faces but we knew it was for different reasons. He stood in front of us and we waited for him to say something but he just shook his head and what we saw in his eyes was shock and deep confusion. We were confused too by what we'd seen because we had no idea what it meant. And then he said in a voice that we could hardly believe was his because we'd never heard it so small and so empty:

"She put her hand in my shorts and she grabbed me. She grabbed my willie and she rubbed it."

Jillie never came to see us again.

Chapter 10
Our Hill Bully Rules

Thinny Hayward was our Hill bully. He didn't just all of a sudden become our Hill bully; he kind of had to earn the position. I know it sounds pretty strange because bullies don't normally have to apply to become bullies. That could lead to a lot of problems, like who would you apply to and who would be qualified to review your application? So, I have to explain.

It all started with Jay Jay, like a lot of things did on the Hill. Thinny was a couple of years older than us kids, older even than Stan but not nearly as big, which was important since that was to be a crucial factor in the development of Thinny as a respectable bully. When it came to how he looked, well, from a bully point of view Thinny had everything going for him — he was an ugly boy. Everyone who ever saw him always said the same thing — "Oh my, that is an ugly boy." And it didn't help any that his favourite expression was an evil scowl that just emphasized his ugliness.

So he had the ugly part down pat, but when it came to the other important part of being a bully, size, Thinny was sadly lacking. Now, he had the height, he was taller than any of us, maybe even as tall as Stan, but from a weight point of view he was as skinny as he was ugly. So we all called him Skinny, but we did that behind his back because you never could tell how someone as ugly as Thinny would react if you called him that up close where he could hear you.

Then one afternoon coming from school we happened to walk by Thinny, who was leaning against a power pole picking his nose and flicking snot balls into the road. Just to be polite, at least that's what he said afterwards, Jay Jay gave him a smile and said "Hey, Skinny, what's happening?" In a flash Thinny jumped out into the road, waved his long skinny arms and made a grab for Jay Jay. We all ran like bats out of hell, as my father would say, until we were a safe distance away, far enough so that he had to yell at us to explain that he wasn't skinny, he was thin.

To call him Skinny, he yelled, was an insult. It implied that he wasn't getting enough to eat at home, and that was also an insult to his mom, who was a really good cook. Except maybe for cassava pie and sometimes leg of lamb which, he had to admit, she often overcooked and sometimes burned. Other than those main things and maybe just a few other little problems she had with codfish and potatoes on Sunday mornings and fish in general and okay, peas and rice and stewed chicken too, she was a pretty good cook, better than average anyway. Just because his mom had a few cooking problems, however, didn't give anyone the right to insult her by calling him Skinny.

"So just remember that," he said, "and don't let me get a hold of any one of you kids because then you're going to find out just how bad, how really bad this skinny kid can be."

And of course it was Jay Jay who had to say something about that.

"Look, you just said something that I don't understand. You got really mad at me for calling you Skinny and yet you just called yourself a skinny kid. How do you reconcile the fact that you can call yourself skinny but I can't?"

We didn't wait around to even wonder what 'reconcile' meant, we just saw the expression on Thinny's face and took off as fast as we could. Even Jay Jay was smart enough to know that it wouldn't be productive to wait for an answer to his question and he actually passed us he was moving so fast. Although Skinny didn't catch us that time none of us wanted to know how really bad that skinny kid could be, so we called him Thinny from then on.

Well, that was the start of Thinny's bullying career, and since every neighbourhood had its own bully we were kind of proud and happy that we had one of our very own too.

And Thinny really worked hard at the job. For example, he used to jump out of the alley by his house when we kids were going home from school, screaming at the top of his lungs. Then we'd start screaming too and running as fast as we could with Thinny chasing after us. But Thinny's mom had given him strict orders as to how far he could go from his back yard, so the chasing, the yelling and the screaming would last only until we were out of Thinny's allotted range.

So Thinny's reign of terror continued, and culminated in the day he finally caught one of us. That one, of course, was Jay Jay. Thinny grabbed him by the arm and after the first few minutes of terror and wriggling, with Thinny shouting "Now I got you, now I got you," very loud in his ear, Jay Jay finally gave up and waited for his horrible, awful fate to unfold. The rest of us stood a safe distance away and waited too, scared and at the same time fascinated by the terrible things we knew were about to happen to Jay Jay, and really glad it was Jay Jay the terrible things were about to happen to and not us. It was also important to see what it was we'd have to seriously avoid in any future confrontations with Thinny.

So we waited for something to happen and that's when it got kind of strange because while it was clear that Thinny had certainly gotten Jay Jay, it soon became equally clear that he didn't know what to do with Jay Jay now that he'd been 'gotten.'

And so we waited and watched the expression on Jay Jay's face change from fear to confusion and then to something resembling disgust, until finally he looked up at Thinny and said "Come on, man, you gotta do something besides saying 'I got you, I got you,' which between you and me is very difficult to reconcile with your nasty threats and unpleasant demeanour." As I mentioned before, Jay Jay learned a lot of words from his comic books. He didn't know what they all meant, of course, but he'd noted the context in which they were used and applied them in real situations where he thought they might fit. But there was that 'reconcile' word again, and judging from Thinny's reaction to it before, we knew that now the real torture was definitely about to begin.

Thinny looked down at Jay Jay and snarled and shook his head and we waited with our eyes bulging out and our hearts beating like bongo drums and our hands over our crotches. I don't know why we all did that but Stan told us one time that it was probably a natural reaction to ensure the preservation of the species. Oh man, sometimes he was worse than Jay Jay.

But after all that, the only thing that happened was that Thinny grabbed Jay Jay by the other arm too, shook him a little bit and shoved him away toward us.

"Get going, " he yelled, "and don't let me get a hold of any of you kids again, because then you're going to find out just how bad, how really bad I can be."

This was all very fine and good, but we all realized that this was almost an exact repeat of Thinny's previous terrible threat, except this time the threat didn't feel so terrible at all. And as we all stood around looking at Thinny looking back at us we all realized something else as well — we had a defective bully. Thinny was not a bully we could be proud of and we knew that something must be done.

So we told Stan about our problem and he promised to help. See, Stan was immune to being bullied because of his size and everything. In fact, when we had the crisis with Thinny we started considering who else we could get to be the Hill bully and we all thought of Stan, but then we figured that wouldn't work too well because we needed Stan to protect us from the bully, and if Stan was the bully who'd protect us from him? So that idea died pretty quickly.

Anyway, Stan suggested that we should all get together and make up some Bully Rules, a list of things we wanted Thinny to do and not do if he was going to be our Hill bully. When we had the Bully Rules done Stan said he'd sit down and talk with

Thinny to give him the Rules and get his agreement.

We got together on the back porch at my house for a Round Table Discussion about what we should put in the Bully Rules. We called it a Round Table Discussion because we all read Jay Jay's Classic Comics about King Arthur and his knights being heroes and all and sitting down at a round table to decide how to rescue damsels and fight and kill their enemies and we liked the idea so we decided to do the same thing.

If we were going to have a Round Table Discussion it had to be about something really important, because only really important things deserved to be discussed at one of those. Except we didn't have a round table, we actually just sat down in a circle and each person made one suggestion, which we'd discuss for a while and then the next person took a turn. Jay Jay went first because if he didn't then when it was his turn he'd always say he was going to say the same thing that someone else already said. Stan said he only did that so he wouldn't have to tire himself out by thinking, so we always made him go first.

After a while Jay Jay came to attach a great deal of importance to going first, and once when I started to make a suggestion before him he got really mad and I didn't see a new *Wonder Woman* comic for a week. So Jay Jay was always allowed to go first, but only in the Round Table Discussions. In all the other meetings he was treated like anyone else in the Gang, except maybe Stan, who was really the leader.

So we made our list and came to an agreement with Thinny. He wasn't allowed to punch, pinch or squeeze too hard, or really hurt us in any way. In return whenever the subject of bullies came up with the kids from the other neighbourhoods we'd all brag about how tough, mean and ugly our bully was and they'd do the same. Probably because our imaginations were fuelled by a steady supply of weird comics, courtesy of Jay Jay, the descriptions of our bully were always much more terrifying than any of the others. Besides, we always went with Thinny's strong point, one that we knew no other bully could come close to matching — we put a lot of emphasis on ugly.

And so everything was going fine. We let Thinny catch one of us every now and then, there'd be a lot of hollering and screaming and acting terrified and he'd give us a light punch or a tap on the head and then he'd let us go. We spread the word all over Pembroke Parish about how lucky we'd been to escape a fate which would have been far worse than death, worse even than losing your favourite bongy at a marbles game.

And then the inevitable happened, something we should have thought of but hadn't, something so obvious to any kid in any neighbourhood in Pembroke. See, if we said our Gang had the fastest runners we had to prove it by having a run-off against the kids in the other gangs. If kids in another gang said they could swim faster or dive deeper than anyone in our Gang they'd have to prove it in a swim-off or a dive-off. It was the same with cricket, with football, with peeing for distance and duration and with farting. There always had to be a contest to see who was best, and we should have seen this one coming.

And it came - the Bully Challenge. Word of our bully and his meanness and his toughness and his ugliness got around to the other kids, all right, but it also got around to the other bullies. Now, this wasn't like any regular challenge, this challenge didn't come from any kids in any of the other neighbourhoods. It came from Omar, the Spanish Point bully, the only bully with a reputation as mean, as terrible and as frightful as Thinny's. But there was one awful difference — Omar came by his reputation honestly.

The place and the time for the challenge was set — Bernard Park just across from the tennis courts at ten o' clock on a Saturday morning when we knew no one would be using the courts, because hardly anyone ever did no matter what day it was. That was because the tennis courts were in such bad condition that it was better to hit tennis balls against the side of your house in your backyard. Also, Bernard Park was so big that we could easily find a part of it where no one was watching because with a challenge like this, we didn't want anyone involved except the kids from the different gangs and Thinny and Omar. Grownups were definitely not invited.

There were three categories in a Bully Challenge — Ugly, Scary, and Mean.

Ugly came first and Omar took one look at Thinny and gave up on that one right away. A win for Thinny in the first category, and it was just us kids in the Hill Gang who knew that was the only one he'd win.

Next came Scary, and with his size and scowl and crooked-toothed, evil grin Omar won pretty easily over Thinny, who tried to capitalize on his appearance by looking uglier that he really was. But since that wasn't possible because he was perfectly ugly to begin with and since he'd already won that category we couldn't vote for him as the scariest. Okay, we actually would have if it had been all up to us but there were too many kids from the other gangs who would have figured we weren't being fair. It really didn't matter 'cause we knew that Thinny was going to lose anyway and it wasn't worth getting in a fight over it. Besides, we were outnumbered.

Then came Mean, and we knew we were doomed. All our bragging, all our lying, all the things we said about how incredibly nasty our Hill Bully was were going to come crashing down on our heads. We were going to be laughed at, scorned and teased for years, maybe until we were grownups and probably even after that. Remember, Bermuda is a really small island, only twenty one square miles, so some juicy stories never died; they just went around and around those twenty one square miles forever. We knew that the story of our Hill Bully was going to be one of those.

Omar went first and took full advantage of his size and awesome power. He leaped toward us, shouting and screaming and we scattered in terror in the face of his glowering meanness, his awful grin and his horrible, crooked teeth. He waved his arms about trying to catch one of us and finally caught Simon, one of the smallest kids from the Pond Hill Gang, and raised him right off the ground.

Simon squirmed and wriggled and begged Omar to put him down because Omar was squeezing his arms really hard and it was hurting him a lot but Omar didn't put him down or stop squeezing him and Simon started crying and tears streamed down his face and he peed his pants. Omar kept on grinning and threw him down so hard he bounced and rolled away with pee running down his legs and into the grass. Simon crawled off and sat by himself and put his head down and cried some more.

Omar smiled like the bad guys did in the *Durango Kid* serials just before they shot the sheriff or some other good guy. Then he looked at Thinny and said, "Your turn" and Thinny started walking toward Simon and we all held our breath and got scared for Simon because we figured Thinny was going to try and out-mean Omar. But when he reached Simon he just bent over and took his arms and raised him up and said, "You go on home now and get cleaned up." Then Thinny came back and walked right by us and headed up toward the Hill.

"Sissy!"

There wasn't a worse thing in Bermuda, maybe in the whole world, that you could call someone and that's what Omar called Thinny. Everything went quiet. Nobody moved. We waited for what we knew was sure to come, waited for Thinny to stop and come charging back, waited for the fight and we knew it was going to be a bad one.

But there wasn't any fight because Thinny didn't come charging back. He just turned and smiled at Omar and kept right on walking.

"Sissy," Omar said again, and laughed real loud. And that's when Jay Jay stepped in front of him and said kind of softly but clear enough so we all heard every word, "He's not a sissy and you're nothing but a sorry-assed bully." Jay Jay said afterwards he'd gotten the 'sorry-assed' part from his dad when he was talking about some work a carpenter had done at his house. He thought that under the circumstances it was an entirely appropriate use of the term, even though he figured it might get him killed. It almost did.

The look of surprise on Omar's face changed pretty soon to shock and then to anger.

"What did you call me?"

And Jay Jay, still looking to be killed, said, " I called you a sorry-ahhh..." which was as far as he got because Omar's hand was around his neck and it was squeezing, hard. We watched in fascination as Jay Jay's face started to turn a weird purple colour, which we all knew from reading Jay Jay's comics would have been blue if he'd been white.

And then Omar let him go, not because he was afraid he might be killing Jay Jay, not because he'd developed a sense of remorse for what he was doing to Jay Jay, but because of the blow on the back of his head. The sound was so loud you could have heard it across the road in the Pembroke Church graveyard. It might not have wakened any of those dead people, as my dad used to say, but it would have come pretty close.

Omar staggered and looked around to see what struck him and another blow caught him in the right eye. He put his hands up to his face and the next one hit him in the stomach so hard he vomited and fell down on his knees. Then Thinny started slapping him up side his head, first one side then the other until he started to cry, and Thinny said over and over again, "Nobody bullies the Hill kids except me, you got it, nobody bullies the Hill kids except me, you got it?" And he was saying it in time with the slaps and Omar kept trying to duck the blows but wasn't having any luck. Tears streamed down his cheeks and snot ran out of his nose. His lips were bleeding and his eye was closed and finally he peed his pants too.

Then Thinny stopped slapping him and said, "You got it?" and Omar nodded his head as fast as he could and through lips that were now all swollen and split he muttered, "Yes, yes, I got it, just don't hit me anymore, Thinny, not any more."

And Thinny didn't hit Omar any more, he just looked at him and shook his head. He glanced over at us, nodded at Jay Jay and said, "You kids go on now or you're going to miss the serial." He started walking away again, stopped, turned around and said "And by the way, don't let me get a hold of any of you kids next week because then you're going to find out just how bad, how really bad I can be."

We left the park and Thinny and headed down Cedar Avenue toward Opera House, and though we were quiet and no one said anything for a long time we all had one thought in our minds: 'Our Hill Bully rules!'

Chapter 11
Monty

My Granny had a dog named Monty. He wasn't a thoroughbred or anything like that. He was a mixture of several different varieties, like Campbell's soup, my dad used to say. I asked her how she got him and she said he came from the dog pound a long time ago. She went there with a friend of hers because someone told her that a good dog could be a real help to a blind person. I asked her why she picked him and she said it was easy, nobody else wanted him and if she didn't take him they were going to put him down.

"Put him down where?" I asked.

She smiled and said it was just an expression that people used to make what they were going to do to Monty sound better.

"What were they going to do to him?"

"Do you remember when you went to the hospital to get your tonsils out and they gave you something to make you go to sleep so it wouldn't hurt when they took them out?"

"Uh huh."

"Well, that's what they were going to do with Monty. They were going to give him something to make him go to sleep, except that it would make him go to sleep forever."

"They were going to kill him."

"Yes."

"His tonsils must have been really bad."

"Actually, his tonsils were just fine."

"Was it because nobody wanted him?"

"That's right."

"Except you, Granny."

"Except me."

"Why did you want him?"

"Well, he licked my hand, and he spoke to me."

"He spoke to you? What did he say?"

"He said, 'Take me', of course, so I did." And she laughed.

So that's how she got Monty.

Monty wasn't a pretty dog. In fact, he was really ugly. He was short and fat with one bent ear and a bob tail. His hair was wiry and short and brown like dirt, with a few yellow patches every now and then to relieve the brownness. His face was ugly too, and although Jay Jay said he heard somewhere that dogs could actually smile it didn't look like Monty ever had a funny thought in his life. If you saw him for the first time you could easily understand why nobody in the dog pound wanted him, at least nobody but Granny.

In spite of the fact that he was short and fat and ugly Monty had one major asset — he was the Long

Leroy of the dogs on the Hill. But the asset could also be a liability because when Monty got excited his willie would grow even longer and harder than it normally was, and sometimes it would catch on the carpet and act like a little anchor, which seriously hindered any rapid forward motion. Monty was a source of endless fascination for my dad. He liked telling people about Monty, although he never called him Monty. He called him Groover, which he explained was because of the grooves he made in the carpet when he got excited.

"Just put a little harness on him," my dad would say, "and a bitch in heat in front of him and he could plough a field." He told everyone he knew about Monty's exceptional 'handicap,' as he called it, although all the men he told, and a lot of the women too, didn't seem to consider it a handicap at all. In fact many of them nodded their heads and smiled and seemed to even envy Monty in some way, which was rather confusing to me.

I think my dad really liked Monty, though, because he often told stories about him. Like the first time he was over to my Granny's house when he was courting my mom. Granny invited him over for supper. Not to be polite, my dad explained, it was just to check him out. That was when he first met Monty.

Apparently Monty wasn't impressed with my dad and headed under the table as soon as supper was served. Granny cooked a real Bermudian dish — peas and rice and curried chicken. But the peas in peas and rice aren't peas at all, they're really beans, and beans always made my dad fart. In fact when he ate beans there generally wasn't what you might call an interval between the eating and the farting. Dad used to be particularly proud of the fact that his metabolism, as he explained it, was so finely tuned that by the time the second forkful of beans was going into his mouth the first one was already coming out the other end, in a manner of speaking.

So you can see what happened at Granny's dinner. The beans in the peas and rice made dad want to fart, and it wasn't long before 'wanting to' became 'having to.' Inevitably 'having to' turned into actually farting, which he tried to disguise by raising a bum cheek and channelling the noise in another direction. 'Something like a fart ventriloquist,' he used to say. After the first fart or two Granny got disgusted and ordered Monty to get out from under the table.

"Monty, get out from under there."

This caused my dad to smile in relief because with Monty being blamed he was free to fart at will. So he let out a few more and after every one Granny would say; "Monty, get out from under there."

Finally, after one particularly noisy fart Granny raised up the tablecloth, reached under the table and grabbed Monty by the collar. "Monty," she said, "get out from under there before that man shits on you."

Man, my dad used to enjoy telling that story. Of course it wasn't true, at least not all of it. Granny would never have said "Shit." She'd never say anything that even resembled a swear word. But I know my dad and I know that if he ate beans that night he would have farted at Granny's table and he really would have tried to blame it on Monty. Which is probably another reason Monty never liked him.

My dad also said that if Monty was a man every woman on the Hill would be after him, even some of the married ones. I think it must have had something to do with his willie because it sure couldn't have been his looks. As I said, he was the worst looking dog on the Hill. That didn't matter to us kids, though, because Monty could do one thing we'd never seen any other dog do — he could climb trees.

He only did it to get at the cats that climbed them to get away from him — the ones that lived. Monty hated cats and when he caught them he killed them, and he caught a lot of cats. Most of them were strays that roamed the Hill and killed birds just for the fun of it so we weren't really bothered by Monty's killer instincts; in fact, we thought it was pretty cool — a tree-climbing dog. We'd have charged the other kids at least tuppence to watch him do it too, except it was too unpredictable. I mean, how could you tell when a suicidal cat would appear?

We had the job of burying his victims down in the bushes because Monty wasn't into carting them away and hiding them anywhere. He was a disdainful warrior who always left them where they lay. So we'd go down into the bushes and dig a hole, drop in the cat and cover it up. One time we actually dug a hole and found that we already buried a cat in it. After that we put a stick in the ground over each grave so we wouldn't make the same mistake again, and we made the cat graveyard a bit bigger to accommodate the growing number of victims. You can see that not only did we have stray cats on the Hill, but they were pretty prolific as well.

My auntie tried to stop Monty from killing cats but her heart really wasn't into it because she hated cats too. She was really allergic to them and just the sight of one would get her sneezing and wiping her eyes and that would last long after the cat had disappeared. So she sort of scolded Monty every time he added another cat to his collection but secretly I think she just did it for appearances sake, to make it seem like she actually felt bad about the cruel fate that befell any cat that crossed Monty's path.

It didn't fool Monty at all, and he continued to do his best to control the cat population on the Hill. We figured that if it wasn't for Monty the Hill might have been overrun with feral cats, and feral cats were evil hunters. They would have made it very difficult to find a wild chicken for our boil ups down in the bushes. So that was another reason we not only supported Monty's ventures but encouraged them as well.

Monty lived until he was sixteen or seventeen, although nobody seemed to know for sure because even Granny didn't know when he was born. We just knew he was real old for a dog. As he got older his hips started to sag and my dad told everyone who'd listen that it was only logical, considering the weight they had to handle. Then eventually Monty's legs started to go too, the back ones, and it was new material for my dad. We thought it was just from old age but my dad said it was actually from supporting his 'equipment,' and any animal that had to carry that amount of weight around for so long would definitely have trouble with its legs. He was just surprised they'd lasted as long as they did considering the strain they were under.

When Monty died my dad built a box to bury him in. It was just an ordinary plywood box but it had one special feature. He cut a round hole in the bottom about the size of an old English penny, maybe a little bigger. We decided to bury Monty under one of his favourite trees just down the Hill a bit from the house. I took the box and dad carried

Monty and the shovel and when we got to the tree dad dug the grave.

He made it big enough so that it could easily hold the box, and he also made one part of it deeper than the rest, sort of a hole in the hole. He put Monty in the box and carefully turned him over so he was lying on his stomach, then he put the box in the grave. He moved Monty around a little bit, like he was adjusting him, then he stepped back, nodded slowly and said it was just about as perfect a fit as you could get.

We put the top on the box and dad shovelled in the dirt until the box was completely buried. On the way home I took dad's hand and told him he was right about the fit, for Monty the box was just long enough and just wide enough.

Dad looked down at me and smiled. "Yeah, son" he said, "that too."

Chapter 12
The Leaning Game

My dad was outside up on a ladder putting plywood over all the shutters on the windows. My mom opened the hatch to the water tank and filled a couple of buckets, some big pots, the kitchen sink and the bathtub. My auntie was busy collecting candles and matchsticks and putting them in a cardboard box with some flashlights and batteries on the counter by the sink. My uncle was gathering up all the yard tools, the lawn chairs, the patio table and anything else that could move and wasn't too heavy, and stacking them in the wooden shed at the bottom of the property. My sister was in her bedroom hiding her dolls under her bed and stashing what she called her valuables in the bottom drawer of her closet behind her underwear and her pajamas.

Me and Stan weren't doing anything. We were watching and waiting, waiting for what was coming. And we knew exactly what was coming. You could feel it —anticipation, nervousness, concern, all of it just hanging around like a fart in the air, as my dad used to say. And we knew that at this time of the year only one thing could cause grownups in

Bermuda to act like that. One thing that worried, bothered, even scared almost everybody on the island. One thing that Jay Jay said united every Bermudian in their fear and trepidation (he didn't know exactly what 'trepidation' meant but he knew it was bad); one terrible, terrifying thing with one terrible, terrifying name — Hurricane.

Terrible –uh huh. Terrifying — sure. Except to every kid on the Hill. We loved hurricane season. We waited for hurricane season. After summer was over it was the absolute best time of the year and the biggest disappointment of all was when hurricanes passed us by and all we got was a storm or two or maybe just some gales.

But we knew from listening to the radio and the conversations the grownups were having and all the phone calls from relatives and people on and off the island that there was no way this hurricane was going to pass us by.

Three words, words that grownups spoke almost in a whisper, words just loaded with fear, with gloom and with doom. For grownups. For us kids, we would have shouted those three words out as loud as we could if we hadn't been afraid of being boxed up side our heads by the closest adult hand. Three words that for all the days leading up to this day had all us kids almost peeing our pants with joy and excitement. Three words that meant we were in for the absolute best thing a hurricane could bring to the island of Bermuda — A Direct Hit!

Everybody knew about a hurricane. That it doesn't hit all at once with all its might and all its power. There's a buildup. The winds increase from strong breezes to gales to storms and then finally to full hurricane force. And it gets noisier and noisier, the sound of the wind whistles and screams so loud that if you're outside you can't hear yourself talking, not even if you shout. And just when you think the wind and the noise are never going to stop, they do. Complete silence, complete calm. You're in the eye.

But before the eye came along and before each of us went home and got inside 'for our own safety', as every mom insisted, we Hill Gang kids performed the most important ritual of the whole season — we played The Leaning Game.

We all lied to our parents and said we were going down to Jay Jay's house to look at his comic books and we'd be sure to be back before the winds and stuff got too bad. Jay Jay told his parents he was going up to my house to look at my comic books and he was sure to be back before the winds and stuff got too bad. But actually what we all did was get together on a narrow little lane just below my house, a lane that ran alongside the top of a cliff that formed one side of an old stone quarry my dad said hadn't been worked for over forty years.

There were five of us — Jackie, Jay Jay, Stan, me and Arnold. Arnold was there for a really good reason. Arnold liked to eat, a lot, and his mother liked to feed him, a lot. Arnold was about five feet six inches tall and three and a half feet from belly button to bum, as my dad said. He weighed twice as much as Stan and three times as much as me. Arnold was there for one strategic reason — he was our anchor.

We got off the lane and walked out very carefully to the edge of the cliff and gave each other room to spread our arms. The wind was building up, getting stronger and stronger, but it wasn't time yet. So we waited and grinned with excitement and yelled above the rising sound of the wind about who was going to be the bravest and go the furthest. And all along we knew that when you were going to have 'A Direct Hit' what we were all waiting for was definitely going to come.

And come they did. Winds. Powerful winds, heavy winds, winds from the northwest, the best winds of all because when they came from that direction they hit all of us standing along that narrow ledge above the cliff right in the face. The best thing of all was the two types of wind that you got with a hurricane - sustained and gusty. And it was the sustained part that was the most important because we needed it to play the Leaning Game.

We spread out our arms and we held hands with the ones next to us. I was at one end of the line and held on to Stan's hand, and he held on to Arnold's and Arnold held on to Jackie's left hand and with his right hand Jackie held on to Jay Jay, who was at the other end of the line. So there we were, in one straight line, arms spread out. Jay Jay and me only had one hand to hold on to because we were at the ends of the line. Stan and Jackie held onto two hands, but the most crucial factor was Arnold.

We needed his grip to be the strongest because he had to hold on and stay back and not do what the rest of us did next. Because what we did next was lean out over the cliff and let the strength of the wind keep us from falling, using Arnold's body to keep us safe if anything went wrong. And with the strong winds and big, round Arnold holding on we knew that nothing could go wrong. Nothing ever went wrong.

Except that just as we were leaning out as far as we could the wind whipped up an ugly, red hornet from a nest on the side of the cliff and blew it directly up into Arnold's nose. Then things happened really fast. Arnold let go of Stan's hand and Jackie's hand and started snorting and blowing and coughing and honking into his two hands that were now not holding on to anybody.

Then an amazing thing happened. We didn't fall over the cliff. The wind was so powerful, so steady it held us up, and when we realized we weren't going to go crashing to the bottom we let go our other hands and just lay into the wind. It was like floating, like flying, and when the wind gusted it pushed us backward so that sometimes we ended up on our bums on the other side of the lane. But then we'd just get right back up and stagger against the wind out to the edge again.

I almost made it to the edge for the third time when all of a sudden I was flying backwards once more, which was kind of strange because none of the other kids were. My feet were off the ground and I had this choking feeling around my neck and when I looked up all I saw was my mom's face and all I felt was her hand around my neck and all I heard was her yelling at me which must have been really loud because I could hear every word pretty clearly above the sound of the wind and none of them made me feel like everything was going to be all right.

I guess she was saying the things that any good mom would say if good moms swore like my dad did when his favourite cricket player got bowled out for a duck at Cup Match last summer. I think that the swearing was because she was scared that the wind might suddenly ease up and I might end up falling about twenty five feet to the bottom of a stone quarry that hadn't been used for over forty years. Then all of a sudden I couldn't hear the wind anymore. I couldn't hear anything except two dull thuds followed by a sort of bell-like sound in my head because she had let go my neck and used her free hand to box me up side both my ears. Hard.

The other kids stopped leaning over the edge and turned around to see what else my mom was going to do to me. They were all grinning and feeling good about this new development because they knew their parents were too far away to get involved in what was obviously going to be a really bad situation for me.

And just as they started to laugh when they saw my mom flatten my ears the wind dropped. It was just a tiny, little lull before it picked up speed again but it was enough. It was Jay Jay who went over, of course, still wearing the grin on his face as he fell, but there was confusion in his eyes and just before he disappeared from view confusion turned to fright.

And I did what any normal kid would do seeing one of his best friends flying through the air like a bird, even if he was flying straight down the cliff. I laughed. It was definitely worth the smack up side my head. But Jay Jay was lucky, because when the wind started up again at full force it blew him right up against the side the cliff and he sort of bounced all the way down to the bottom.

So everything worked out pretty well in the end for Jay Jay because he only broke one arm, and after they put a cast on it in the hospital he was a real hero on the Hill. Since it was Jay Jay doing the talking the story got bigger and better. Soon everyone who took the time to listen heard about how he broke his arm when the hurricane slammed him up against the cliff; how he fell like a stone almost one hundred feet; how he miraculously survived by heroically grasping at tree roots and branches with his one good arm while the other hung loosely and uselessly at his side; and how this slowed his descent just enough so that he landed at the bottom on his two feet as gently as a feather.

Chapter 13
Mr. Hunt is Singing His Song

Christmas Eve. For us kids on the Hill it was a time of joy, a time of excitement, a time of happiness and a time of fear and nail-biting anxiety. We knew that Mr. Hunt was going to try again this year, as he did every other year that we could remember, and we knew that this year he was going to try harder than ever, as he had every other year that we could remember. And he always said the same thing: "This time he won't escape. This time his head will roll."

We knew of course he wasn't talking about a Christmas turkey. We all got ours from the Portuguese farmer up in Paget two days ago, with their feathers all plucked and their guts all cleaned and their heads already chopped off. No, the head Mr. Hunt was talking about rolling belonged to that one visitor all of us had been waiting to see for one whole year — Santa Claus.

And so each year we gathered in Mr. Hunt's back yard looking like the outlaws in the Opera House movies who'd been condemned to the gallows, and feeling like them too. We went there because we wanted to see if he really was getting ready to kill

Santa Claus. And Mr. Hunt would wait until we got there and then he'd grin and go into his shed and come out with his axe and whetstone. He'd sit down on his porch step and sharpen the axe and then he'd sing his Christmas song. And in spite of all the carols and all the jingles and all the Christmas songs on the radio every day leading up to Christmas we just couldn't get Mr. Hunt's song out of our heads, mainly because there was only one line to it and he repeated that line over and over:

"You better watch out, you better not pout, you better not cry I'm telling you why" - then he'd pause and look around at each one of us and grin an awful, evil grin and sing in a whispery, scary voice — "Santa Claus is dead." Then he'd sing it again.

Every time we shook our heads and told him there was no way he was going to catch Santa, that he never caught him any other Christmas and that Santa was just too smart for him. We said it again and again but it was really more to make us feel better than it was to convince Mr. Hunt, because there was always a chance he was right, that this was the year Santa would make a mistake, that he wouldn't be fast enough to escape Mr. Hunt and his wicked axe, and that worst and most unthinkable of all, he'd be dead before he could deliver our presents.

Of course, even though we always told our parents what Mr. Hunt was planning it never seemed to bother them very much. They'd smile the smile that all parents smile when they think their kids come up with really stupid ideas, and they'd tell us not to worry because Santa always comes and if he was killed how were the children all over the world going to get their presents?

This didn't make a bit of sense to us, first of all because we didn't care if children all over the world got their presents as long as we got ours, and second because it seemed pretty obvious that if Santa got himself killed then all those children all over the world just weren't going to get any presents. And neither would we. That was the problem as we saw it, but apparently not one parent on the Hill was the least bit concerned.

As usual Jay Jay was the one who alerted us. He ran up and down the Hill shouting as loud as he could so that every kid in the Gang could hear: "Mr. Hunt is singing his song! Mr. Hunt is singing his song!"

So we all went to see Mr. Hunt and as usual he was waiting for us in his yard. We stood silently while he went to get his axe and the whetstone, while he sat and grinned and scraped the stone over the razor edge of the axe. Then Jackie asked a question that none of us ever asked before, although once he asked it seemed pretty obvious, so the rest of us started to nod and go "Uh huh" as if it was on the tip of our tongues to ask the same question but Jackie just beat us to it.

"Mr. Hunt, why exactly do you want to kill Santa Claus?"

The question seemed to surprise Mr. Hunt, and the sly grin disappeared from his face. Then something very strange happened. He stopped sharpening the axe and put it down on the step. Then he put the whetstone next to it and looked up at Jackie. But it wasn't so much that he was looking at Jackie, it was more like he was looking through him at something else, something that none of us could see, something that wasn't really there.

When he spoke his voice was different from before. It was soft like a whisper and we had to lean forward and be really quiet to hear what he was saying.

"Why do I want to kill Santa Claus? That's a good question." Then he was quiet some more and that far away look came into his eyes again and when it went away he said, "And it deserves a good answer. An honest answer."

This time he looked directly at me and his eyes weren't far away at all.

"I was about your age," he said, "maybe a little older. We lived up in Friswell's Hill, just like you used to do, and Christmas, oh my, Christmas was the best time of the year, the very best time."

He reached down and picked up the axe and turned it so that the sun shone off the blade.

"See this axe. It's old, almost as old as me. Passed down to me by my Pa, well, sort of. He didn't really pass it on to me and I'll tell you why in a minute. But this axe was really important, especially at Christmas. Any of you want to take a guess why that was?"

"Sure," Jay Jay said right away, "It's because your Pa was going to use it to cut off Santa Claus's head too. See," he said, turning to the rest of us, "it runs in the family."

Mr. Hunt smiled and shook his head.

"No, Jay Jay, that's not why it's important. It's important because every year my Pa used this axe to cut down our Christmas tree. Every morning on Christmas Eve he'd go out into the shed and get this axe and hone it to the sharpest edge he could get with this stone right here. Then he'd take me by the hand and we'd go into the woods and he'd find the tallest and fullest cedar tree there was, and then he'd climb way up into the branches as far as he needed to and take this axe and cut the top of that tree right off. And that was our Christmas tree, and it was always the best Christmas tree in Friswell's Hill. And Pa would always say "That's Santa Claus's tree, and we have to get the best Christmas tree every year so Santa Claus will keep coming to the house, 'cause if we don't he's just gonna stop coming and that'll be the end of Christmas." Then he'd laugh out loud at the expression on my face and give me a hug and say that was never, ever gonna happen because we'd always have the best tree.

So every year Pa would climb the tallest cedar tree and chop off the top for Santa Claus, and every year the kids in the neighbourhood would gather around at the bottom all excited and happy and cheering, right up to the Christmas Eve when Pa slipped off a branch way up in a tree that was slick with cedar gum and fell about fifteen feet right down among us kids.

Now, I know that fifteen feet isn't too big a drop, and things probably wouldn't have been too bad if Pa hadn't landed right on this axe, which he was still gripping in his hand and which went right into his chest and killed him dead. As you can probably figure we didn't have a tree that year.

Ma took it really bad, went a little funny in the head, to the point where she couldn't really look after me and my sister so we went to live with my Granma. It was only supposed to be for a while until Ma got better but she never really did get over what happened so we stayed with my Granma basically for good, because next year in the spring Ma took the bus down to Crawl, walked through the bushes over to Abbotts Cliffs and jumped off."

It was about as quiet on the Hill as I can ever remember. We just stood there staring at Mr. Hunt, not daring to say a word because none of us knew what to say. We didn't really have any experience with grownups dying and here was Mr. Hunt presenting us with two of 'em in a row.

Mr. Hunt was quiet too, looking away again into the distance, out toward Dockyard across the water, but I don't think he was looking at Dockyard at all. He sighed and hunched his shoulders and he stopped looking at something that must have been very far away and set his eyes on me once more.

"Anyway, Santa Claus didn't come that year, or any more after that. It was like my Pa said: 'No tree, no Santa.' He came to the other kids in Friswell's Hill but he didn't come to us. Not really. I mean, we got presents and candy and things like that from some of the neighbours and cousins and uncles and aunts, and sometimes my Granma would lay out some presents and pretend that they came from Santa Claus but she never fooled us. We knew that Santa Claus would never come again. Like I said, he came to all the other kids in the neighbourhood but not to us."

He paused and pointed his finger at me. "I was about your age, or maybe a little older, when I decided that Santa Claus was just a mean old bugger, and that even though my Pa died trying to get him the best Christmas tree of all time Santa Claus just didn't care one little bit, not one little bit. So that's when I decided that Santa Claus had to die too, and I was going to take this axe, the one right here that killed my Pa, and I was going to use it to kill Santa Claus."

Mr. Hunt stopped talking and looked at us staring at him with eyes open so wide we couldn't blink, and he ran his hand along the handle of the axe and his fingers along the blade. Then he put it down again, shook his head.

"But you know something, I never could catch him, never could. He was always one step ahead of me, always gone before I got there, like a bloody ghost."

He grinned then, not the sly, sneaky Christmas Eve grin we were used to seeing when he normally talked about Santa Claus but a different one. For some reason that different grin made us all relax, and we breathed a little better and moved a bit so we didn't look like a bunch of little brown, wooden statues. Jay Jay relaxed so much that he farted, and when we looked at him he just shrugged and said "I had to let it go. I've been holding it in forever, waiting for the right time, and it seemed like there was a lull in the story so...."

Jackie looked at Mr. Hunt and said "Wow! You mean every year since you were six, or maybe a little older, you've been waiting on Christmas Eve to kill Santa Claus?"

"Well, not every year. It took me a while to decide that's what I was going to do, then of course I had to take a pretty long break once I found out that there really wasn't a...". He stopped suddenly and looked up at us listening to and absorbing every word he said.

"As I was saying, once I found out there wasn't much chance of getting my hands on that old bugger. Yes indeed, Santa Claus is one wily old fella, almost impossible to catch."

"So why'd you start up again with the axe and stuff?" I asked.

"Well, seeing as you kids were so wrapped up with Santa Claus I decided that the only way I'd get any kind of revenge on the old fella was just to have some fun with it, and it was easy, because you kids are all so gullible." He smiled and shook his head, got up and took the axe and the stone and started walking toward his shed.

"Truth is," he said, turning back toward us, "I'm never going to catch old Santa Claus. He's been around way too long and he's way too smart for me." Then he looked at the axe in one hand and the stone in the other and sighed. "Guess it's time to put these away for good," he said, and went into the shed.

On the way home I asked the other kids about something that had been on my mind since Mr. Hunt said it.

"What's gullible mean?"

Stan and Jackie shook their heads. Arnold started to say something but then he shook his head because it was pretty obvious he didn't know either. Jay Jay did.

"I know exactly what it means. I saw it in one of my Classic Comics. It has something to do with going on voyages to really strange places where the people are either huge giants or teeny little midgets no bigger than ants. There were even places where horses were the rulers and they could talk English."

Stan sighed and refrained from going up side Jay Jay's head.

'Does this have anything, anything at all to do with the question, Jay Jay, which was, by the way, 'What does 'gullible mean?'"

"Of course it does. The Classic Comic. It was all about this guy named Gullible, and he was the one who travelled to all those places."

"Where horses talked and giants and ant people lived."

"Yeah, that's him."

"And you believed that?"

"Well, kind of," Jay Jay said and looked down at his feet.

"It's okay, Jay Jay," Stan said, and chucked him on the arm. "Hey, we all believed that Mr. Hunt was going to kill Santa Claus too but as Mr. Hunt said, you can't kill Santa, and we should have known that. He's gonna be around forever." He shook his head and sucked his teeth.

"We're so stupid", he said. "No wonder Mr. Hunt figured we were just a bunch of little Gullibles."

Chapter 14
How We All Began

Screwing. Although none of us had ever done any screwing and didn't have any idea about what was actually involved in screwing we'd all heard about it. It seemed to be really important, especially to the older teenage boys because they talked about it all the time. But it was something they told us kids in the Hill Gang we were too young to understand. When we were older and bigger, they said, then we'd find out what it all meant. They kept the details to themselves, like screwing was some big, mysterious secret that could only be revealed when you were the right age and the right size - obviously when you got to be a teenager.

So naturally, because nobody would tell us and all the teenagers kept it a secret, we couldn't wait to find a way to learn what screwing was all about. And Jay Jay made us even more curious after he told us it must be really important because as he understood it, screwing had something to do with how we all began. I asked him 'How we all began what?' but he looked at me like I should know what he meant and said 'Began. Began being kids'. This answer didn't make sense to any of us and he knew it. He just shook his head and said he wasn't sure how it all fit together but his cousin Norman told him that, and Norman knew all about it because he had a whole bunch of kids and he said that screwing was really important in how all of them began.

This got us even more confused so we figured we'd go to the one place that we knew held all the answers, but Jay Jay said it wouldn't do any good. He already looked in his trunk and searched through all the comic books and there was nothing in any of them about screwing and how we all began. And so it was one of those things that kind of stayed in the back of our minds, but not too far back, and we knew we needed to get more information at the first opportunity.

And then we had a real breakthrough, and it actually did have something to do with Jay Jay's comics and his cousin Norman. One day when we were down at Jay Jay's house looking at his newest *Wonder Woman* and *Mandrake the Magician* comic books Norman dropped in to see Jay Jay's mom about fixing her toilets. Norman was a plumber and he fixed all the toilets on the Hill. Jay Jay said it was an opportunity we couldn't let slip because who knew when his mom's toilet might overflow again and Norman would be back? It could be months, he figured, and now that he was right here in the house we should ask Norman to tell us what he knew about screwing.

All we needed was someone to go get Norman and tell him what we wanted. We knew that this wasn't going to be just an ordinary mission because of the importance of the issue, and we knew that whoever went to get Norman might seriously run the risk of getting smacked upside his head for even bringing up the subject of screwing, because it was obviously so mysterious and so secret that kids our age shouldn't even be thinking about it. So we did 'Eeny meeny minie moe' until I got chosen to get Norman.

I went out into the kitchen and Norman was sitting on a chair drinking a St.Pauli Girl beer and eating a fish sandwich. I waited for him to finish the sandwich and just stood there until I knew he'd start to wonder why I was just standing there looking at him eating and then he'd ask me what I wanted and then I could sort of just take it from there. He kept eating his sandwich and drinking his beer until he finished the sandwich.

"You gonna stand there all afternoon or you gonna tell me what you want? And I know you're not hungry because you just had your lunch a while ago and you're too young to be looking for a beer, so why're you standing there staring at me like a damn owl watching me eat?"

"Um um, we ... well, Jay Jay wanted to ask you some questions, and we wondered if you could come down to his room so he could ask you them."

"So Jay Jay's got a secretary now? You his secretary delivering his messages? Well, Mr. Secretary, why didn't he just come on out here and ask me his questions himself?" He said this with a smile on his face and I knew he figured out that something was up and I thought maybe the hard part might be over.

"Well, actually we all wanted to hear the answers. To Jay Jay's questions."

"Jay Jay's questions, huh?" He smiled some more and got up and I followed him down the hall to Jay Jay's room.

"Jay Jay, I hear you've got a bunch of questions for me."

Jay Jay threw me a look, the kind you give to a traitor or someone like that, but I shrugged my shoulders. "I was only supposed to get him, and I got him."

"Yeah," Jay Jay said, "but the questions were ones we all had, not just me."

"But Norman's your cousin so you should be the one to do the asking," Stan said, and we all nodded and Jay Jay knew he was elected. Norman stood there with a smile on his face and the St. Pauli Girl in his hand, waiting.

Jay Jay took a deep breath and moved across the room away from Norman, out of 'smacking up side the head' range.

"Okay," he said, looking around at us for support, "we have a couple of questions and we all thought that you were the best person we could ask to get some answers."

Norman took a sip of beer, nodded his head and kept on smiling.

"Well...um, it's about...it's about...um...okay, it's about screwing." Jay Jay jumped back a bit after saying 'screwing' so Norman couldn't reach him too easily, just to be on the safe side. But Norman just smiled some more, drained his beer and said "Ahhh." Then he sat down on the top of the comic book trunk and said, "What exactly about screwing do you want to know?"

When we saw that Norman wasn't going to get mad or start smacking anybody we all spoke up at once, until Norman held up his hand and said "Okay, one at a time," and he pointed to me. "You first, since you're the smallest."

That somehow made me feel important, though I don't know why. I'd long ago found out that being the smallest in the Gang was not necessarily an advantage, but I wasn't going to let this opportunity go by.

"Jay Jay said that you said that screwing was important for how we all began and we hear the big kids talk about screwing but they won't tell us what it really is and we figured that since you were a grown up and told Jay Jay that it was important you could tell us what it was. Maybe." I stopped because I was out of breath.

Norman went over and closed the bedroom door. He came back and sat on the trunk again and put his empty beer bottle on the floor. He looked each of us in the eye and none of us moved. We hardly breathed. We knew we were about to hear one of the greatest secrets of life, right here in Jay Jay's bedroom.

"You all got willies, right." Norman said, which was more of a statement than a question but we all said "Yes" anyway.

"Well, one of these days you're going to find out that willie of yours is gonna be used for more than just peeing through and playing with. It's gonna get a little hard and stiff, if it doesn't do that every now and then already, and you're gonna want to grab it and put it somewhere."

We all just stared at him until Jay Jay asked the question that was puzzling all of us:

"What do you mean 'put it somewhere'? It's attached."

Norman shook his head and looked disgusted. "You don't have to worry about that, Jay Jay, you're gonna put it somewhere while it's still attached."

Now we were really getting interested and excited too, because 'where we all began' involved something we were really familiar with, something each of us had indeed peed through and occasionally played with — a bit. Just a few times. Oh boy, there were more things we could do with our willies than we thought and we were eager to learn what they were.

"Okay, kids," Norman said, "here's the bottom line, the most important part of the whole issue." He paused and the room went totally quiet. We were holding our breath in anticipation because at last it would all be revealed. We were going to find out where we all began and most important, we were going to find out the secret of screwing. And then Norman spoke the three words we would never forget.

"It involves girls."

And then we understood why no one would talk to us about it, why the big kids thought we should wait until we got older because they knew by then we'd be able to handle the news a whole lot better. We knew the secret might be bad but we didn't think it would be this bad. But Norman had said it and Norman should know — if you were going to get involved with screwing then somehow, someway, you had to get involved with girls.

We stared at Norman, too shocked to speak. Norman saw our expressions and he grinned and then he laughed. "It's not that bad, kids," he said, and he laughed some more.

"Just wait, when you get a little older you'll find that girls are going to be a real interesting part of the whole process."

And then he got up off the trunk, picked up his beer bottle and left the room.

Chapter 15
Caught

Granny exercised almost every day. She did every exercise ten times. On Mondays, Wednesdays and Fridays she did ten Knee Bends, ten Bend Over and Touch your Toes, ten Jumping Jacks, ten Sit Ups and ten Push Ups. In between each set of ten exercises she took a thirty second rest, then she did them all over again two more times. On Tuesdays, Thursdays and Saturdays she'd do Side Bends, Leg Raises, Sit Ups and Running on the Spot for two minutes. They were her easy days, she used to say. She never exercised on Sundays because she said if God could take a break after working all week, she sure as heck could take one herself. She used to smile and wink when she said that so in case God was listening he'd know she was just kidding.

Whenever I was home at exercise time it was my job to count the thirty seconds between exercises, and when I got to thirty I'd say "Go," and she'd start on the next set. I used to do exercises with her sometimes but I could never keep up with her. I was only a kid and she was better at it than me — after all, she'd been exercising a long time.

Granny was over seventy years old. I was always curious about how old she really was but she never would tell me, no matter how many times I asked. The only thing she ever said was, "I'm as old as my tongue and a little older than my teeth." It made sense, I guess, but it didn't help me much.

One time I asked her how long she'd been exercising and she said she started as a young girl, about as old as me, back on Grand Turk in the Turks and Caicos Islands where she was born. She didn't know exactly why she started because there was nobody there to teach her how to do the exercises, and in school all they did was play cricket and football, and only the boys did that. The girls just played hop scotch and skipped rope. Basically she developed the exercises for something to do and because she felt good after she did them. She was way ahead of her time.

Anyway, when she grew up she came to Bermuda with her husband. She had three children, my mom, my auntie and my uncle. When Granny got diabetes and went blind her husband left home and never came back. I never met him because my mom was only sixteen when he went away. He didn't want to be stuck with three kids and a blind wife because he thought he might have to do a lot of work raising the kids and looking after Granny.

He didn't know Granny because if he did he would have stuck around. She may have been diabetic and completely blind but she raised her children on her own and my mom said she did as good a job or better than any two parents who could see. I thought that anybody who'd leave his wife just because she was blind and they had three kids to look after wasn't worth knowing anyway so I was glad I never met him.

The funny thing was that no one ever talked about him. It was like a forbidden subject, except no one ever said it was forbidden to talk about him since no one ever talked about him. It was like he never existed. I never, ever had the nerve to ask Granny about him and she never mentioned him. I never even knew his name. It was like he'd come down from outer space and then gone back again. One time I asked Stan about him and he said the only thing he knew was that he once heard my dad tell his dad that 'the bastard had gone to Canada, to Montreal'. I hardly ever thought about him. To me he wasn't my grandpa. He was a ghost, and just as dead.

A couple of times, though, especially when she was doing her exercises, I was tempted to ask Granny if he exercised too, and if he did was it because people used to kick sand in his face on the beach in Turks Island like they did with Charles Atlas in Jay Jay's comic books. I was hoping that was the case because I liked the idea of people kicking sand in his face.

Granny played the piano. I knew a lot of blind people played a lot of different instruments and if they were blind they usually were really good at playing. Bermuda had some blind musicians who were really well known, like Lance Hayward and Jean Southern. And then there was Ray Charles over in America, and everyone knew about him.

All those blind people were really good. Granny wasn't. She didn't play the piano very well even though she was blind. Granny used to sing while she played the piano. She sang hymns, mostly, and she sang a lot better than she played. I used to like to stand by the piano bench and watch her play and hear her sing because she used to enjoy herself so much. She sang very loud and you could hear her even if you were outside and the doors and the windows were all closed.

She had favorites like "In the Garden" and "Lead Kindly Light," and before I was three I knew the words to all her songs because I heard them so often, and every Sunday for sure. We used to do duets together, too. I sang soprano and Granny sang bass, and everyone said we sounded pretty good.

Apart from singing hymns on Sunday Granny listened to the church services on the radio. She never got strange about them, and never, ever asked me to listen to them with her or tried to get me all religious and stuff. She was never that way herself, except she always listened to the radio services on

Sundays, to one in particular, and that one was Oral Roberts and his broadcast from Oklahoma in America.

One of the main reasons she listened to him was because he was supposed to be a faith healer and after he finished his sermons he took some time out to heal a few folks. It was better for being healed if you were right there in the church with him, because then he'd tell you to come on down to the front of the church where he was and he'd start to heal like crazy, laying his hands on people and making them walk if they were lame and run if they were slow. He cured headaches and measles and all sorts of things and you could hear the healed people on the radio sighing and clapping and thanking him and Jesus and God and everyone in sight while the congregation sang and chanted and generally made a lot of happy noise. But the part Granny waited for every single Sunday was when he finished with the people in the church and turned all his powers to those people listening to him on the radio.

He told all the sick and infirm people (I wasn't too sure what 'infirm' meant but it didn't sound good) out in the world listening to him to put their hands on their radios and then he'd start to yell out, "Heeeyull, heeeyull, in the name of God I order you to be heeeyulled." I don't know how many people out in the world actually got healed by putting their hands on the radio but Granny used to do it regularly.

Mr. Roberts would finish his sermon, she'd turn up the volume and put her hands on the radio. Mr. Roberts would yell "Heeeyull! Heeeyyull" and when he finished Granny would still be blind. But Granny never lost faith. Every Sunday she turned on Oral Roberts and every Sunday he told them to put their hands on the radio and every Sunday Granny did it and every Sunday Mr. Roberts yelled out "Heeeyull! Heeeyull!" and every Sunday Granny would still be blind.

But Granny knew that sometimes the healing process might need a bit of a nudge, so after every unsuccessful attempt to heal her blindness she gave me a shilling to send to Mr. Roberts so that he could continue to tell her to get healed in the name of God. As she said, you never could tell when the breakthrough might come, and it wouldn't do to have Mr. Roberts off the air just because he didn't have the funds to carry on.

I didn't think that her shilling was going to make a lot of difference to Mr. Roberts or increase his yelling to people to make them get better and make Granny see again, but I never said anything about my doubts. I just took her shillings and put them in a sock in my drawer. On her birthday I took them out and went with my mom into town and bought her a present with them, usually a can of Planters

Mixed Nuts because she loved them. After her birthday I saved up the shillings again until Christmas and then I bought her another can of Planters Mixed Nuts. I figured if she couldn't get healed she could at least get nuts.

But sometimes being blind wasn't such a bad thing, especially if the blind person was your Granny, because then you could get away with some things you couldn't get away with if she could see. One of those things was the Planters Mixed Nuts, which she really loved, and which I really loved too. Granny used to find different hiding places to keep the nuts, like in the middle drawer of her dresser on the left hand side in the back behind her stockings and underwear. Or in a shoe box under her bed as far in as she could reach.

She must have figured that no one would find them in her special hiding places, that they'd be so well hidden they'd be safe from any little kid's prying eyes or fingers, mine in particular. What she didn't know was that after I gave her the nuts I'd walk away so she could hear me going down the hallway, and when she thought I was far enough away I'd sneak back up without making a sound and watch where her new hiding place would be this time. Then I'd just wait until she left her room to do something in the kitchen or maybe play the piano or take Genghis for a walk and I'd hit the nuts. But I wasn't greedy or stupid and I only took a few at a time so she wouldn't notice or remember how many she'd actually eaten.

But as usual, I underestimated Granny's intelligence and overestimated mine.

Genghis Khan was our new dog, a German Shepherd we'd gotten to replace Monty. The people we got the dog from were moving off the Island and Genghis needed a good home. They were friends of my dad and dad knew that we needed a dog and that's how we ended up with Genghis Khan.

Dad's friends gave him that name and Jay Jay said he figured it was because Genghis was really a mongrel and not a German Shepherd at all, and the people who'd owned him before named him that because he was a mongrel and everyone knew that Genghis Khan was the famous king of the Mongrels a long time ago on some vast and endless plains.

"It's pretty obvious when you think about it," Jay Jay said, and since he was the only one of us who'd actually thought about it we took his word for it. I asked my sister about it because she was a lot older than any of us kids in the Hill Gang and knew a lot about all sorts of things, even for a girl. She rolled her eyes and the first thing she said was "Did Jay Jay tell you that?" She usually rolled her eyes and said the same thing whenever I asked her something that actually did come from Jay Jay. Then she explained the difference between mongrels and Mongols and said I should take everything that

Jay Jay said with a whole box of salt, never mind the grain, because his entire education outside of school came from comic books, and comic books weren't the *Encyclopedia Britannica*. My sister didn't have a very high opinion of Jay Jay or his comic books.

Even though my dad was responsible for us taking Genghis Khan he didn't really like him as much as he liked Monty, which was kind of funny because unlike Monty, Genghis really liked my dad. Whenever my dad was around Genghis would run up to him and wait to be petted. Dad would give in after a while and pet him a few times but we all knew his heart wasn't really in it and he did it just so Genghis would go away.

I wondered why dad didn't like him since Genghis was a nice, friendly dog, but I heard Mr. Hunt talking about it one day with my Uncle and they were having a good laugh. Mr. Hunt was telling my uncle that since Genghis wasn't hung like a horse like Monty was, my dad didn't have anything to focus on. It wasn't that he didn't like Genghis, Mr. Hunt said, it was just that as far as my dad was concerned, after being around Monty for so long he found that Genghis was just plain boring.

Anyway, after a while Granny and Genghis became best friends and we walked him nearly every evening, as long as it wasn't raining or we were having a storm or a hurricane or something like that. Granny particularly liked the fact that Genghis was just an ordinary dog, 'with ordinary equipment,' as my dad once said, so she was really glad she didn't have to listen to any comments about his 'equipment,' except for sometimes when my dad was talking to his friends and compared it with Monty's.

We were out walking Genghis on a warm evening exactly one week after her latest birthday, in which, according to her, she, her tongue and her teeth became one year older, although her teeth still remained just a little younger than her tongue. She always took my arm and we'd go down the driveway and across the lawn and when we got back we'd walk up the steps to the porch and sit down in the armchairs and talk. We talked about all sorts of things, mostly about what I'd done during the day and what I planned to do the next day. She always wanted to know about school and what was happening there, and sometimes she brought a book outside and I'd read to her for an hour or so. She really liked that. Then we'd talk about what I'd read.

She liked Shakespeare and we talked about him a lot, although I didn't understand most of what he wrote because it seemed like a lot of his writing wasn't even good English. There was a lot of 'thous' and 'thees' and words that nobody used any more.

There was a big difference between him and Jay Jay's comic books, although Jay Jay did have some Classic Comics and one of them had the story of Romeo and Juliet. I never read all of it because it was about love and kissing and hanging off balconies. When we teased Jay Jay about it he said it wasn't his fault because it came in a bunch of Classic Comics his aunt Audrey bought him. His mom wouldn't let him put them in the trash because his aunt Audrey was one of those people who thought it was never too early for little kids to learn. She said that Classic Comics, which included books like *Ivanhoe* and *Quo Vadis* and historical things like that, were a really good starting point.

But Granny seemed to understand Shakespeare's stories pretty well and she spent a lot of time explaining what they meant, especially the ones with wars in them, which were the ones I liked best. I really didn't understand most of the explanations but I read his stories anyway because she really liked them and I really liked her.

"I'm really enjoying my mixed nuts," she said, and I told her I was really happy that she liked them.

"And how about you?" she asked.

I was kind of confused. "How about me what?"

"How about you? Are you enjoying my mixed nuts too?"

Caught. Just like that, and I didn't understand how.

I had to confess. There was nothing else I could do. She knew, and she knew that I knew that she knew.

"How'd you know, Granny?" I asked in as sheepish a way as I could manage, mixing in some sorrow and guilt so I could get as much sympathy as possible. Granny was too smart to fall for it and I got a real good lecture on stealing. If it had been my mom or my dad the lecture would have been accompanied by several smacks up side my head, timed to emphasize every point, especially when it got to the shame part. It would have been "Shame!" — smack. "Shame!" — smack. "Shame!" — smack, with a whole lot of 'You should know betters' and a bunch of 'You haven't been brought up to steal from anyone, let alone your own grandmother!' thrown in. I think things were so bad that if it had been my dad I might even have gotten the belt. But thank goodness it wasn't.

Granny never, ever boxed my ears, smacked me up side the head or strapped my bum when I did wrong. She just talked gently, quietly and softly and when she talked I listened and when she finished I'd feel worse than if she actually boxed my ears, smacked me up side my head or strapped my bum. I'd also have learned my lesson. Even if sometimes the learning only lasted for a week or two, and sometimes maybe only for a couple of days. But the lesson about stealing her nuts lasted forever.

"How did you know, Granny?"

"It was very simple. I saw you."

I couldn't believe she said what I thought she said.

"You saw me?"

"Oh yes. The very first time. You were so cute, walking down the hallway so noisily to make sure I heard you going, then walking back so quietly to see where I put the nuts."

I was still thinking about what she said first. "You said you saw me. Granny, you're blind, you can't see. You can't see a thing."

"Oh shush, child, of course I can see. I see with my hands, I see with my nose, and I especially see with my ears, and when you came tiptoeing back to my room I could hear you and I could smell you."

I tried to remember what day of the week it was when I sneaked back to her room. Saturday night was bath night so if it had been a Saturday, or even a Thursday or a Friday, smelling me might not have been a problem. I wasn't really worried too much about smelling, though. It was summer and I was like every other kid in Bermuda. I spent half the time overboard and if all that salt water didn't get you clean, bath water sure wasn't going to do the trick. And everybody knows that no matter how high the temperature is kids don't do something that all grownups do — kids don't sweat.

But I still wanted to know.

"What do I smell like, Granny?"

She put her hand out to touch my face, as she always did when she wanted to tell me something important. I think it was just to make sure I was listening.

"Today you smell like you, but with just a touch of summer. Sea salt and sun, I can smell it on your face and in your hair."

"But you said I smell like me and that's what I want to know. What do I smell like?"

'Tell me, child, exactly what does an orange smell like, those big, fat, juicy Bermuda oranges? Or how about the peaches your auntie grows in her backyard garden. What do those oranges or peaches smell like?"

I tried really hard with that question, really hard, but the harder I tried the harder it was to think of an answer. But Granny was smart — she knew there was no answer and she knew that I'd figure it out, and I did

"An orange smells like an orange, and a peach smells like a peach, and I smell like me."

"Yes, that's absolutely true, and there's one other very important thing to remember. Only an orange smells like an orange, only a peach smells like a peach, and only you smells like you."

And I understood then exactly how I'd been caught.

Chapter 16
Fried White Grunts

"Hey," I said, "did you guys remember? It's been almost a year."

Jackie looked over at me. "A year?"

We were in the Oleander Fort on the side of the Hill, me and Jay Jay and Jackie and Stan and Arnold. We were sitting on stools we'd made out of old pieces of cedar logs, having a rest after a tough game of Cowboys and Indians with the St. John's Road Gang from down below the Hill. We figured we'd won but they said they had too and we argued about it for a while. We knew before we played Cowboys and Indians they had a football game with the guys from Spanish Point that they didn't want to miss and that if we argued long enough they'd give in. After about ten minutes they did and finally agreed that okay, maybe we did win.

The Oleander Fort was just one of a couple of forts we built on the Hill, and we needed more than one because if there was any kind of a storm or even a gale it was pretty much a given that at least one of our forts would blow down.

The Oleander Fort had already lasted four months, mainly because we built it right inside a big patch of oleander bushes. We used an old machete that Stan's dad threw in a drawer in a cupboard in the back of the yard shed because it was too rusty and dull to be of any real use to him. It was fine for what we needed and after a lot of hacking and chopping we cut a path leading into the middle of the patch. Then we did more hacking and chopping until we made a space big enough for all of us to sit down and conduct any Hill Gang business that needed to be conducted.

It wasn't the biggest fort we ever built but it was one of the best, with oleander branch walls so thick you couldn't even see inside it, except in a few places where if you were a rival gang member and you really tried hard you might, just might, be able to spy on us. So we cut down some Match- m'Can branches and filled up those holes.

All of us knew that Match-m'Can bushes were really named 'Match me if you can'. But we didn't have the time or the patience to call them by their real name, so for us and almost every other Bermudian they were Match-m'Cans. They were called that because people said the leaves were like the stars — no two were exactly the same.

We knew it was impossible to match any of the leaves but some people kept trying all the same. It was really foolish to try and although you'd tell them it was useless and kind of stupid some of them still kept trying. Especially tourists.

I remember one day when a lady came up the Hill and stopped to look at a Match-m'Can bush. I was walking up the Hill behind her and she must have heard me because she turned around and said, "Hi there."

I knew right away she was a tourist because a Bermudian would have said "Good afternoon." Bermudians never said "Hi there." If it was early in the day they said "Good morning." Late in the day they said "Good evening", and at night they said "Good night." So in the afternoon if you met someone, especially someone white and tanned wearing brand new Bermuda shorts and they said "Hi there," you knew it was a tourist.

"Good afternoon," I said.

She smiled and shook her head and said,

"I'm sorry, I should have known better. After all, I read the guide book. Good afternoon, sir."

I liked her right away — she called me 'Sir."

I stopped and she pointed to the Match-m'Can bush and said "Is this the plant with no two leaves exactly the same?"

I nodded.

"Uh huh. And you should never, ever try to match them."

"I wouldn't dare. It'd be like trying to match two snowflakes. That's impossible too." Then she smiled at me and started off down the Hill. After a couple of steps she stopped and turned back to me. "Thank you, kind sir," she said, "and good afternoon."

I didn't know anything about snowflakes but I knew she wasn't foolish, even if she was a tourist.

I smiled, remembering her and thinking she probably would have liked our Oleander Fort with the Match-m'Can patches.

Jackie got up off the log he was sitting on and went out through the opening and we could hear him peeing in the bushes. When he came back in he looked at me again. "Hey, I had to go, and remember what your dad always says: 'Pee anywhere but don't pee your pants.' Anyway, you were saying something about 'one year'"?

"Uh huh, one year tomorrow."

Jay Jay of course couldn't hold back. He put up his hand like he was in school, waving it around until he had everyone's attention.

"Hey, I know, I know. You're right, you're right. It was exactly one year ago tomorrow."

"You remembered, Jay Jay?" I was really surprised because Jay Jay hardly remembered anything that didn't directly concern him or his comic books.

"Course I did. It was the Saturday me and my uncle Danny went fishing out on Challenger Banks and I caught that giant blue marlin and ..."

Stan leaned over and smacked him up side his head hard enough to make him shut up but not really hard enough to hurt.

"Jay Jay, you went fishing with your uncle about seven months ago. It wasn't on a Saturday at all, it was a school day and you played hooky because you knew your uncle Danny was just worthless enough not to tell your mom. And you didn't go anywhere near Challenger Banks. You just anchored out by North Rock and nobody caught any giant blue marlin, least of all you. What, did you forget I was on Devonshire Dock after school when you guys came in and I saw it all? It was your uncle who caught the biggest fish, and that was only a red hind. The only thing you caught was a couple of breams!"

"Shit bibblers!" Arnold shouted, "You went fishing all day and all you caught was some shit bibblers!" Then we all started to laugh because every kid on the island knew that the most useless fish in Bermuda waters was a bream, that breams ate nothing but garbage and that their favourite food was poop. At least that's what every kid in Bermuda grew up believing, mainly because that's what everyone who ever fished off the rocks or off a boat in Bermuda told them.

Granted, none of us ever saw a bream actually eating poop, but that didn't mean that they didn't. They were nice looking fish with a big black spot by their tails, but nobody I knew ever ate a bream, or ever would. After all, they ate poop and nobody wanted to eat poop, even if it was second hand. So most of the time we didn't call them breams — they were shit bibblers.

"So Jay Jay," Stan said, "considering that this has nothing to do with you or your shit bibblers, why don't you just keep quiet and listen?" Then he pointed to me.

"So what was this thing that happened exactly one year ago on Saturday?"

Everybody looked at me and I felt my eyes water up and I took a breath to make sure I didn't stammer because I knew what I had to say was important, really important.

"David drowned."

Then all of us got real quiet and you could hear the hum from the Electric Light Company way down on Serpentine Road and the cicadas singing on the cedar trees around the fort.

"So should we do something?" Arnold said, breaking the silence. "We should do something, right?" We stared at him because usually the first person who said anything to break any silences that happened in our gang was Jay Jay. But he was still a little concerned about Stan who was sitting next to him, and he wasn't ready to test whether Stan's order about keeping quiet still stood.

"Maybe we should say a special prayer, you know, pray something in his memory," Jackie said quietly.

"No way." Jay Jay hadn't said a word for more than five minutes, which under normal circumstances would have been a record for him, but even the threat of a smack from Stan couldn't keep him quiet any longer.

"No way," he said again. "Prayers are for church and funerals and we already prayed a whole lot when they buried David. Besides, we don't know any special prayers and if we tried some new ones I know we'd mess 'em up and then he'd be all mad up there in heaven. And being mad in heaven has got to be a bad thing, right?"

Stan looked at Jay Jay and sucked his teeth and rolled his eyes, but when we thought about it for a minute we had to agree with Jay Jay.

"You know what I think we should do?" I said. "I think we should have a celebration."

Then Arnold got all serious and shook his head.

"I don't know about that. A celebration? You think it's all right to do that, I mean, celebrate and stuff because somebody died, especially if he was our friend? It'd probably be fine if we didn't like somebody and they died but we all really liked David, we liked him a lot."

"We wouldn't be celebrating because he died. We'd be celebrating because when he was alive we all used to have a whole lot of fun when he was with us. We'd be celebrating because he belonged to our Hill Gang; because he played all our games. He was really good at Simon Says, remember, and Rounders too."

"Yeah," Jackie said, "but he always lost at marbles. Man, he was the worst marbles player ever."

Stan gave him a look and Jackie put up his hands. "I know, I know, we have to say good things about him if we're going to be celebrating, but you got to admit, when the games were over he never had a single marble left. On account of him none of us ever spent any allowance on new marbles." Then he looked over at Stan and grinned. "Hey, that's a good thing he did for us, right, a good thing?"

"Sure it was," I said, "and he never got mad when he lost because he knew we were happy to get his marbles and that made him happy too. Same with a celebration. We'd be having fun and he'd know that we were having fun because of him and that would make him happy, just like with marbles, and he'd be smiling and smiling, you know, just like he always used to."

Stan was the first to nod his head and pretty soon we were all nodding and going "Yeah" and "Good idea" and I was feeling really good about my suggestion. Arnold said "What kind of celebration are we gonna have?" and everybody stopped nodding and started thinking. Then Jay Jay put his hand up and waved it around like he always did when he thought he had a good idea. "I know, I know, why don't we each tell a story, our favourite story about him, like the time we hanged him, or when we tied him to Stan's kite and made him fly; or the time..."

"No," Stan said, really loud. "Uh uh. Those are times we took advantage of him, just because he was the smallest and because he'd go along with anything to fit in, no matter what we did to him. No, I don't think those are the kind of stories we should be telling at all."

It was true and we all felt a little bad because even though we tried real hard to think of a time when we hadn't taken advantage of him we really couldn't come up with anything important.

Then Arnold said, "I've been thinking." We knew he was thinking because for the longest while he sat with his elbows on his knees and his chin in his hands and his eyes closed, which was what he always did when he was thinking.

"Okay, what were you thinking about?" Jackie said.

"Vikings."

Jackie said "Uh huh," like Arnold thinking about Vikings was the most normal thing in the world.

"Yes, I was thinking about Vikings. See, when one of their warriors or an important chief or somebody like that died they used to put them in a boat and float it out to sea and set it on fire and burn up the boat and the dead person in it."

Jay Jay shook his head. "Two things," he said. "One, David's already buried and two, we don't have a boat."

Arnold glared at him. "That's not funny, Jay Jay."

"I was only pointing out —"

"Well, stop 'pointing out' and get serious," Stan said. "Go on, Arnold, what were you thinking?"

"Well, I was thinking about Jay Jay's Classic Comic books, and I remembered that the only one of us who ever really liked them and ever read them was David. And then I was thinking that maybe in his memory we could do something like the Vikings used to do. That maybe in his memory we could take all of Jay Jay's Classic Comics, put them in a pile inside the fort and burn them up. That way David would have been the very last person to have read them and nobody else could read them ever again. Burn 'em all, that's what I was thinking."

There was dead silence then, except for a sort of choking sound. It was Jay Jay gasping for breath. His mouth was wide open and he was trying to speak but nothing was coming out. Stan looked over at Jay Jay and smiled and said "Arnold, I think that's a great idea." Which was when Jay Jay got up and put his hand over his mouth and ran out of the fort. We could hear him throwing up in the bushes outside and we knew that burning his comic books was one celebration that wasn't going to happen. Stan went out and we could hear him talking real quiet to Jay Jay and when they came back in Jay Jay was smiling and wiping his mouth.

"A joke," he said, "you guys played a joke on me. Boy, you really had me fooled, really worried for a minute. I even had to go out there and calm down. But Stan said it was all a joke and that's good because it was my auntie who gave me those Classic Comics and I just couldn't burn them up, not even one of them. I mean it wouldn't mean a lot to me, you know, but my auntie...my auntie..." and tears started to fill up in his eyes.

"It's okay, Jay Jay," Stan said. "Arnold was just trying to get your goat, weren't you Arnold?"

And Arnold nodded and went right along with it.

"Sure, Jay Jay, I was just joking, you know we'd never burn any of your comic books."

"Okay then," Stan said and looked around at us. "Who's got another idea?"

"I know what we should do," I said. "I know exactly what we should do."

They looked at me and nobody asked me what I thought we should do. They just waited.

"What we should do is we should all go back down to Forster's Bay and have our celebration down there."

Nobody said anything right away, and then Jackie put up his hand kind of hesitantly.

"Do you really think that'd be all right, to celebrate down there? I mean, that's where he drowned…that's where he died."

"I know, I know, but don't you see, it wasn't just the place where he died, it was also the place, the very last place, where he was alive. That's why we should go there to celebrate. He'd like that, I know he would."

Jay Jay agreed immediately that it was a great idea, mainly because we weren't talking about destroying any of his precious comic books any more, even if he thought the idea was a joke.

"Oh yeah, I think that's exactly what we should do," he said, "Exactly."

"Exactly, Jay Jay?" Arnold said. "If you think it's exactly what we should do, what do you think we should do to celebrate when we get there, exactly?"

Jay Jay thought a bit then shook his head. "I don't know, exactly."

Arnold said "Yeah, right," and cut his eyes at Jay Jay and Jay Jay stuck out his tongue right back.

"Fish fry."

We all looked at Stan.

"Fish fry," he said again, "let's have a fish fry. Remember how much David liked them. I don't know anybody who liked fried white grunts more than him, so that's what I think we should do."

We thought about it for maybe ten seconds, started nodding our heads, and in another ten seconds we agreed.

It didn't take long to arrange. Me and Stan would bring the frying pan, the butter, the salt and the hot pepper sauce and Jackie would take the plastic plates, forks and knives. Jay Jay was in charge of the lemonade and cups and Arnold was responsible for the grill, the matches and the firewood.

Next afternoon we all got together at Forster's Bay. When you went down the narrow trail along the cliff leading down to the water's edge there was an opening in the side of the cliff that was like a small cave with a big overhang in the front. Stan said it had probably been eroded by the wind and rain over hundreds, maybe even thousands of years, just like all the other limestone caves you could find practically anywhere in Bermuda.

He read somewhere that Bermuda probably had the highest percentage of limestone caves per square mile of any place in the world. But he said considering Bermuda was only twenty one square miles in area you didn't need a whole lot of caves to make it a world beater.

Stan said our cave was just one where the entrance wore away and probably wasn't really a true cave, more like a worn-out hole in the wall, a shelter.

With a flat floor and the overhanging roof it was an ideal spot for a fish fry, and kids used it for years to fry the fish they caught off the rocks around Forster's Bay.

The water in Forster's Bay was deep and it was a great place to catch white grunts, squirrel fish and sometimes if you were really lucky you might even hook a nice, big, yellow grunt. White grunts usually ran about five or six inches long at the most, and they weren't nearly as fat as a good yellow grunt. They were so small it was hard to scrape their scales off and clean them so we just fried them up whole, 'guts, skin, scales and all', as my dad used to say. All you had to do was be careful to spit out the guts and the skin and the scales when you ate them. Then of course there were the bones, which in a five-inch fish were extra small and really sharp. There wasn't one Bermudian kid who ever ate a fried white grunt who hadn't choked on at least one fish bone and swallowed dozens of others.

None of that mattered because a white grunt was one of the best-tasting fishes in the world, especially if you caught it and cooked it yourself. Fishing at Forster's Bay wasn't always about catching white grunts, though, because for every white grunt you caught you generally caught at least one - or most times two - shit bibbling breams.

We baited our hooks with suck rocks, which were like barnacles that stuck so hard to the rocks you had to use a knife or a screwdriver to pry them off, and even then you'd break the tip off your knife if you weren't careful. But they were the best bait you could get for grunts. Breams loved them too and so did cowpollies and slippery dicks.

Our schoolteacher told us that cowpollies were really named Sergeant Majors because they were green with black stripes that made them look like the badges some of the soldiers in the Bermuda Militia wore on their shoulders. We called them cowpollies because that's what everybody except tourists and people who worked at the Bermuda Aquarium and our schoolteacher called them. I don't know where the name came from because they didn't look anything like a cow.

We figured slippery dicks got their name because they were long and skinny and covered with a layer of slime, although some of the older boys used to grin and say that wasn't the only reason.

Cowpollies and slippery dicks were smart because they nibbled at your bait until it was all gone. They never seemed to take the hook, and it was unusual to ever catch one of them. That was okay with all of us because nobody ever ate a cowpolly or a slippery dick anyway. It wasn't because they were shit bibblers like breams, it was just that cowpollies were too scaly and bony and slippery dicks felt like they were covered in snot, and while it was okay to eat your own snot nobody wanted to eat something else's.

Breams were not smart fish. They were stupid and greedy and they'd chomp down on the bait and the hook and half the time we spent fishing we'd be cutting the hooks out of them, slitting them open and tossing them back overboard so we could watch them get eaten alive by their brothers and sisters. That was the only fun part about catching a bream.

So on Saturday afternoon we all went down to Forster's Bay to have our celebration. We knew Arnold was the best white grunt fryer of us all, so while he set up the grill and everything in the shelter the rest of us got ready to fish. We unrolled our handlines, tied a small stone on each one about a foot from the hook to act as a weight, pried off a bunch of suck rocks, baited the hooks and tossed the lines overboard.

Jay Jay caught the first fish, a white grunt that was so small you could hardly see it on the hook. He pulled it off and threw it back because he knew Arnold wouldn't fry anything under five inches long. Jay Jay's grunt was about two and a half, although he argued it was much nearer four. He had a problem with estimating fish sizes, but only when it related to anything that he caught.

The water was as clear as glass and we could see cowpollies darting in and out, nibbling at the bait and scooting away when they stole a piece. Every now and then a slippery dick slithered in and tugged a bit of suck rock off one of the hooks. The white grunts tried to bite and run too but they weren't as good at it as the cowpollies and slippery dicks so we were each catching one every four or five minutes. We put them in a bucket of seawater because we wanted them nice and fresh when we fried them.

Jay Jay stared down into the water for a while then he looked at us and said, "Hey, the breams aren't biting."

That was just fine with us because we knew that as soon as they started to bite we'd be hauling up shit bibblers by the ton and it was going to be a while before we caught enough grunts for Arnold to fry.

Slowly the number of grunts in the bucket got bigger and bigger and we seemed to be catching them faster than ever before.

"There's a reason for that," Jay Jay said after a while. "The breams aren't biting."

Stan punched him on the arm. "Shut up, Jay Jay, you're going to jinx the whole thing. Don't worry, shit bibblers always bite, they just haven't started yet."

So we concentrated on fishing. It was a normal Bermuda summer afternoon. The sun shone super-bright, the sky was almost as blue as the water and the water was almost as warm as the weather. If it hadn't been for the celebration we'd all have been overboard, swimming and diving and making the water boil. But today none of us felt like doing any of that because we all remembered what happened a year ago.

We fished for another hour until the bucket was half full of swimming grunts and we decided that there were more than enough and it was time to stop. As he pulled in his line Jay Jay shook his head and whispered almost under his breath, "The breams, they weren't biting. They weren't biting at all."

"I know," I said, smiling, "and I know why."

Then Jay Jay smiled too and soon we were all smiling, because all of us knew why.

We carried the bucket up to Arnold who had started the fire and put the pan on the grill. He reached into the bucket, took out a handful of grunts and arranged them carefully in the pan. They wriggled around a bit when they hit the melted butter but that didn't last long, and soon they turned a nice brown colour and my mouth started to water. Arnold sprinkled on some salt and pepper sauce and turned them over so they could cook on the other side.

After they were done he forked them onto a plastic plate he put on the ground by the grill and took some more grunts out of the bucket. By the time the bucket was empty and all the grunts were fried up our stomachs were growling. We each grabbed a fork and knife and Arnold took out the plates, put five grunts on each one and passed them around. We caught enough of them so that each of us could have as many as three helpings if we wanted. Jackie poured the lemonade, which by this time was luke warm, and we finally started to eat.

"Boy oh boy oh boy," Jay Jay said, with his mouth full of fish and grease running down his chin, "this is the best..." and then he stopped and his whole body shook and his eyes and his mouth opened as wide as I'd ever seen them and he stared out at the cliff.

We turned to see what shocked him so much and there, coming down the path along the cliff and heading directly towards us, was David's mom. We were so stunned that none of us could speak. We looked around, terrified, but there was no escape because the path was too narrow to run around her. So we waited, dreading what was to come but knowing that however horrible our punishment might be, we deserved every bit of it.

We fastened her son to the line on Stan's big kite and flew both him and the kite over the Hill; we tied her son up with the nanny goat rope and tried to hang him from the branch of a cedar tree, and one year ago in this place, in Forster's Bay, we made the water boil while her son sank unnoticed to the bottom and drowned.

She came into the shelter and looked around at our staring eyes, our open mouths and our frightened faces.

"Your mom told me about the celebration," she said to me, "that's why I've come."

I looked at her face and saw the tears in her eyes and I tried to speak.

"Mrs ... Mrs ... Robinson, I ... we're... so sorry for ... for ..." but she put a finger to her lips and said "Shhh, shhh, I think what you boys are doing is just perfect."

And then her eyes leaked and two tears rolled down her cheeks and fell onto the sand. She wiped two others away and reached a hand out to Arnold.

"Could I have a plate too? David loved fried white grunts."

We sat and ate and watched the sun dip down beyond the Dockyard across the Sound, watched the shadows creep across the quiet, still waters of Forster's Bay, and David's voice came to me again and whispered in my ear that this was the best fish fry ever.

And it was.

Later

Over time something happened that happens to most of us. It didn't happen to David but it did to the rest of the gang on the Hill. We grew up.

Jackie joined a calypso band and played the conga drums at all the big hotels and night clubs in Bermuda, and when the entertainment business went downhill he bought a taxi and made a lot more money driving tourists around the island.

Rickie Ratteray went on to play soccer and became one of the best soccer players Bermuda ever produced.

Jay Jay started his own successful pesticide business and fumigated homes from St. Georges to Somerset.

Arnold went to a technical school and became a plumber, made a lot of money and lost it all in alimony payments to three ex-wives, each of whom divorced him after less than one year of marriage.

Stan went to school in Toronto, graduated as an architect and built some of the finest homes and cottages on the Island.

Zack went to medical school and came back to practice at home. When my mother grew old she succumbed to the ravages of Alzheimer's Disease and developed gangrene in her legs from bedsores that were neglected for far too long. Her mind went away, her pain became unbearable, her quality of life non-existent. I spoke with Zack and reminded him of the Pact and asked him to honour it. He did, and my mother passed in peace.

Jillie grew up too, but not too much. When she was thirteen she took a stool and a belt into her parent's room and hanged herself in her father's closet. Her mother left home shortly after that and her father went back to the West Indies amid rumours that weren't really rumours at all.

I left Bermuda and went to university, graduated and now live my life off-island. I still talk to David from time to time, although he doesn't participate in our conversations as often as he used to, and I still return to the Island. When I do I go over and gaze up at the Hill.

And I remember.